Cost-Saving Measures That Until Now Have Remained the Best-Kept Secrets of the Fortune 500 . . .

"The entrepreneur blind to better ideas is on a treadmill. By stubbornly insisting that the experts in taxation, financing, compensation, accounting, marketing, advertising, publicity, and law can teach him nothing, he fails to capitalize on the profit-building loopholes and techniques that are at the cutting edge of business management."

—Mark Stevens

Make a Ten-Minute Appointment on Your Calendar Every Day for

The 10-Minute Entrepreneur

MARK STEVENS is one of this country's most respected business advisors. His syndicated column, "Small Business," appears in more than a hundred newspapers nationwide. He was the writer and producer of the nationally syndicated radio program "Let's Talk Business," is a contributing editor to *Dun & Bradstreet Reports* and *Sylvia Porter's Personal Finance Magazine,* and has contributed to *INC., Venture,* and *Boardroom Reports.* An adjunct faculty member of Pace University's Lubin School of Business, he has lectured and hosted seminars to hundreds of small businesses, professional practices, and major corporations. His business books include the bestselling *The Big Eight,* an inside view of the major CPA firms.

THE
10-MINUTE
ENTREPRENEUR

Mark Stevens

WARNER BOOKS

A Warner Communications Company

Warner Books, Inc., 666 Fifth Avenue, New York, NY 10103

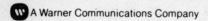 A Warner Communications Company

Printed in the United States of America
First Printing: May 1985
10 9 8 7 6 5 4 3 2 1

Book design by H. Roberts Design

Library of Congress Cataloging in Publication Data

Stevens, Mark, 1947–
   The 10-minute entrepreneur.

   1. Small business—Finance.   2. Finance, Personal.
I. Title.   II. Title: Ten-minute entrepreneur.
HG4027.7.S84   1985   658.1'592   84–21890
ISBN 0-446-38069-5 (U.S.A.) (pbk.)
       0-446-38070-9 (Canada) (pbk.)

Contents

THE
10-MINUTE
ENTREPRENEUR

Introduction

Webster's New Collegiate Dictionary defines an entrepreneur as "one who organizes, manages, and assumes the risks of a business enterprise."

True . . . But another, non-dictionary definition more accurately reflects the entrepreneurial spirit: "Someone who works sixteen hours a day for himself so he doesn't have to work eight hours for someone else."

Meaning: entrepreneurship is essentially a state of mind. It is a determination to accept investment risk, to monopolize decision-making authority, to control economic destiny, and to fuse one's business and personal affairs. Thus the sixteen-hour days.

The typical entrepreneur gives to the business what it demands, regardless of how much work or time that entails. But does that make a successful entrepreneur? Not necessarily.

The wise entrepreneur—the profitable entrepreneur—reverses this, first determining the business's needs and then demanding that they be met. The difference boils down to a matter of *time*. While the typical entrepreneur reacts to his business by ricocheting from one crisis to another, his consistently successful counterpart allocates a portion of his entrepreneurial agenda to anticipating and sidestepping crises, discovering and exploiting opportunities, and finding more effective and enlightened ways to run his business.

"But who has the time? Who can afford to take time away from business to plan and to learn?"

Better question: Who can afford not to? The entrepreneur blind to better ideas is on a treadmill. By stubbornly insisting that the experts in taxation, financing, compensation, accounting, marketing, advertising, publicity, and law can teach him nothing, he fails to capitalize on the profit-building loopholes and techniques that are at the cutting edge of business management.

There are two ways to run a business: by sheer momentum or by cultivating innovative strategies that constantly improve and enrich the venture. For every action the entrepreneur takes, there may be a better, more profitable alternative. *The 10-Minute Entrepreneur* reveals these options and shows how to make them work for you.

How can the entrepreneur use expert counsel to achieve personal success? Example. In the late 1970's, a quiet British real estate developer landed in Manhattan with an idea and a dream. The idea: to build modest-sized office buildings for the New York–based subsidiaries of European corporations; the dream: to challenge Manhattan's established real estate families for a position of power in the city's real estate market.

The Briton, Howard Ronson, has succeeded on both counts, building an extraordinary enterprise (HRO International) with more than five-million square feet of prime office space in its real estate portfolio, and creating a grand personal fortune complete with a chauffeured Rolls-Royce and residences in New York, London, Paris, and Monaco.

Ronson's secret to success is that he approaches his business—his entrepreneurship—as "a manager of consultants." For each of the development process's sub-disciplines such as accounting, law, financing, construction, leasing, and so on, Ronson hires the best professional firms, pays them premium fees, and charges them with the responsibility of safeguarding his interests. Ronson is then free simply to manage the consultants and to indulge in the essential aspects of successful entrepreneurship: creative development of business opportunities and strategic planning to achieve goals.

The 10-Minute Entrepreneur brings to you the sources of management insight and information—the little-known strategies for making and saving money on business ventures. By following the procedures outlined on these pages, you benefit from a team of the leading business consultants and authorities whose ideas and strategies are presented in this book. You learn to capitalize on:

- Loopholes in tax laws.
- Innovative approaches to business financing.
- Cost-saving measures that until now have been used by the Fortune 500, but rarely by small business.

And you learn to implement these strategies within the constraints of sixteen-hour days.

The 10-Minute Entrepreneur is designed to incorporate business-building procedures into the entrepreneur's schedule. By focusing exclusively on simple-to-implement action plans—Quick Fixes—*The 10-Minute Entrepreneur* brings immediate rewards in the form of incremental profits or significant savings. In some cases, the benefits can accrue within twenty-four hours.

How to Use *The 10-Minute Entrepreneur:*

1. Identify a ten-minute period that can be set aside for weekly strategy sessions. Best times are before (breakfast time) or after (at bedtime) the business day. This insulates you from business-related interruptions.

2. Note the allotted time on your appointment diary for each of the following fifty-two weeks, with provisions for doubling up during vacation or travel periods. Every effort must be made to keep the planning period sacred.

3. Refer to the table of contents. Select the subject that interests you most or that you believe speaks to the weakest aspect of your business venture. The chapters are independent exercises that may be read and implemented in any order that is most appropriate for the business.

4. During the scheduled planning period, read the selected chapters twice—first to gain a basic understanding of the Quick Fix and second to make notes on implementing it. Where relevant, jot down addresses and telephone numbers, names of managers, employees, or outside professionals whose services will be required to put the plan into action and the responsibilities you'll be delegating to them.

For example, Chapter 38 reveals how to gain co-op subsidies to cover up to 100 percent of your advertising costs. Note how firms can match small companies with available co-op dollars, steps you can take to qualify for the funds, and instructions for your advertising agency, assistant, or secretary. This is your action plan.

5. Take the action plan to the office, giving marching orders to those responsible for implementing it. In some cases, this may take little more than a phone call.

6. Note on your calendar to monitor adherence to the plan in ten days, and again in a month. Make certain steps have been taken to extract maximum benefits from the Quick Fix.

7. Monitor the results in three months, six months, and a year. If results warrant, schedule a repeat of the action plan.

8. At your next weekly strategy session start the process once again with Step 3, this time selecting the subject of next highest priority.

I

CUTTING TAXES

1

How to Deduct the Company Car

AMERICA'S love affair with the automobile is as evident in the company parking lot as the family garage. For small-business owners, acquiring a company car—or for that matter a minifleet of them—is fringe benefit number one.

The appeal extends beyond the turbocharger and the leather seats. Unlike its family-owned cousin, the company car is a good-looking, fast-moving tax deduction. Expenses incurred in buying and operating a business car can be deducted on personal or corporate tax returns.

But what is the best way to claim this deduction? Is it tax-wise to buy or lease? How much can you spend?

"There is some confusion about how to handle the deductibility of company cars," says a partner with Price Waterhouse, CPAs. "That's because there are several ways of writing them off. Just which one is preferable depends on a number of variables including the type of car being purchased and the projected mileage. In each case, the small-business owner should calculate the costs and the tax benefits of the various options and make a choice based on the numbers."

Tax specialists offer the following guidelines:

• Deductions may be based on the Internal Revenue Service allowance of 20.5 cents per mile for the first 15,000 miles and 11 cents thereafter. Depending on the cost of buying and maintaining the car, this may or may not cover the expenses incurred in operating the vehicle. An alternate approach is to tally all of the costs of ownership—including gas, oil, repairs, maintenance, insurance, and depreciation—and claim this amount as a tax deduction.

• Deductions can only be taken for that percentage of a car's use that is business-related. This includes trips to customers, clients, patients, advertising agencies, banks, and suppliers but not for commuting to work or for personal travel. Tax advisers suggest keeping a detailed diary of all business travel and basing deductions on less than 100 percent business use. IRS examiners tend to believe that most company cars are used for some personal travel.

• Owners of exotic or classic cars may fare better by claiming the per-mile method of deduction rather than by deducting the actual costs of operating the car.

"That's because a key component of actual costs is depreciation, which is generally taken over three years," the Price Waterhouse partner explains. "But with an exotic car, say a collector's item, the IRS may claim that the vehicle will appreciate rather than depreciate and the examiner may therefore disallow the depreciation deduction. Because the per-mile allowance has a built-in depreciation factor, it may be the wiser choice."

• For automobiles costing over $17,000, depreciation must now be stretched out over longer periods.
• Leasing offers no inherent tax advantage as compared to buying. Although leasing advertisements often insinuate certain tax benefits through so-called business and professional leasing, this may be the more costly approach.

"Leasing is just another type of financing," the Price Waterhouse partner adds. "It does not provide a deductible item that is not available through outright purchases. In fact, buyers are entitled to an investment tax credit equal to 6 percent (up to a maximum of $1,000) of the cost of the car. Although lessors may pass this along to their customers, they'll often boost their leasing rates in the process.

"But there are advantages to leasing. Companies can lease cars with little or no down payment and they can do off-balance-sheet financing, which means the transaction does not dilute the firm's debt-to-worth ratio. This can be important when seeking to raise money through bankers or investors."

Adds a vice-president of marketing for Avis Rent A Car, a leading car-lessor, "Another advantage to leasing for companies that don't need the tax benefits is that we'll keep the investment credit and give them lower monthly payments in return."

Seek professional advice for acquiring and deducting business automobiles.

2

Putting Business Property in Owner's Name May Save Taxes

KEEPING business property in the hands of the company owner rather than the corporation can produce substantial tax savings. If properly structured, the write-offs associated with property ownership can shelter salary and other personal earnings.

"All too often, small business owners and professionals put their business property holdings—be it office buildings, stores or other types of real estate—under corporate ownership," says a Hartford, Connecticut-based tax attorney with Cigna Corp., a financial services firm. "This is generally a mistake because the tax benefits can be put to better use by the individual.

"Much wiser is for the principal, who is probably in a higher tax bracket than his corporation, to retain title to the property and to lease it, as an investment asset, to his company or professional practice. This enables him to claim deductions that can reduce his ultimate tax liability."

Major deductible items include:

• Depreciation: Under the Accelerated Cost Recovery System (ACRS), eligible real estate can be depreciated over eighteen years. On a $500,000 building, depreciation deductions for the first two years, for example, are approximately $25,000 and $50,000 respectively.

• Interest: That portion of the mortgage payment that represents interest on the loan is fully deductible. On the same $500,000 structure, a $400,000 mortgage could produce approximately $40,000 in annual deductions during the early years of the loan.

• Property taxes, insurance costs, maintenance and repairs are also deductible on investment property. This could add an additional $10,000 or more to the annual write-offs, producing a total of $100,000 with interest and depreciation.

"Here's how the deductions work in favor of the individual," the attorney explains. "Of the $100,000 in deductions, only $50,000—interest, taxes and mainten-ance—are out-of-pocket expenses. The $50,000 for depre-ciation is not a cash expense to the owner. If he rents the property to his business for $50,000 a year, he'll get sufficient cash flow to cover the out-of-pocket expenses, and the $50,000 depreciation is the sweetener. This can shelter from tax an equivalent amount of salary or other income."

The most effective approach is to purchase business-related property in the individual's name. Once the corporation owns the asset, switching it to the owner or stockholder may be a taxable event.

"A property distribution will likely be considered a dividend, which is taxable to the individual as ordinary

income and possibly as a capital gain to the corporation,"
the attorney adds. "This can wipe out the benefits of
changing over to personal ownership."

But not always. Sometimes, it pays for the individual to
buy the property from the corporation and to accept the
immediate tax consequences in order to gain the long-term
advantages of personal ownership. A classic case is where
the property has not appreciated significantly and the
corporation is in a substantially lower tax bracket than the
owner. In this situation, there may be much to gain by
shifting the tax benefits to the business owner.

But there are caveats.

"While we generally advise our clients to take personal
ownership of business-related property, the arrangement
must be structured so that it is not viewed solely as a tax-
avoidance scheme," says a CPA with the accounting firm of
Margolin, Winer & Evans. "This means the rent should be
based on fair market value and there should be opportunity
to benefit from the property's appreciation."

Additional caveats pertain to the company's balance
sheet and the owner's estate planning. By replacing an asset
with a lease obligation, the company may diminish its debt-
to-worth ratio and thus be less attractive to lenders. And
separating the property from the business may complicate
the division of assets by the owner's heirs.

"Still, you can always switch property from personal to
corporate ownership simply by making a non-taxable
capital contribution," the tax attorney explains. "So it's best
to start off in the individual's name and should there be
some need to change, it's much easier to put the asset into
the corporation than to remove it.

"I tell my clients, if they're thinking of buying a
property in the name of their company or practice, think
once, twice, three times and still don't do it."

Review the options with a tax adviser.

3

Adjusting to Tax Law Changes

S WEEPING changes in the nation's tax laws—now almost as common as congressional elections—force business owners to rethink a wide range of management practices. Two such laws, the Economic Recovery Tax Act and the Tax Equity and Fiscal Responsibility Act, have complicated once simple decisions on acquiring and deducting business assets.

"ERTA and TEFRA have generally reduced the capital gains tax rates and have substantially shortened the number of years over which the cost of real and other property can be depreciated," says a partner with Peat Marwick Mitchell, CPAs. "The investor can now realize a greater return on certain investments after taxes, this being known as the after-tax rate of return or ATROR. This fundamental change mandates a reevaluation of certain business policies."

The CPA offers the following guidelines:

• Selling or Exchanging Real Estate. Property owners seeking to acquire larger business facilities have often used a tactic known as "like-kind exchanges" to reduce the taxes on property dispositions. Rather than sell their store, warehouse, or office building—and pay taxes on the appreciated value—they exchange it for new property, simply adding cash or notes to meet the higher purchase price.

"While exchanges used to be the best approach in most cases, the new tax laws may favor a sale and purchase," the CPA advises. "Accelerated depreciation now enables owners to write off real property in eighteen years rather than over its useful life, which could spread over forty years or more. This accelerated treatment is allowable only for purchased property. In addition, because the capital gains tax for individuals—and this includes proprietorships and partnerships—has been reduced from 28 percent to 20 percent, there is less tax due when the appreciated property is sold.

"This means that in most cases only those with a high ATROR in the property should still do exchanges. For others it is probably better to sell, pay the capital gains tax and take the benefit of the faster write-off. For example, an individual in the 50 percent bracket with an ATROR of 8 percent will save over $5,000 for every $100,000 of gain by selling rather than exchanging his property (providing 80 percent of the property's value is in depreciable structures). Conversely, the same individual with an ATROR of 20 percent would be about $4,000 ahead by exchanging."

• Expensing or Capitalizing Assets. Traditionally, business owners have been advised to deduct, whenever possible, the cost of business assets (including automobiles, furniture, and appliances) in the year of purchase, thus gaining an immediate tax saving. But the tax law changes make this less of a knee-jerk decision. Again, except for those owners with a high ATROR and a high marginal tax rate on personal or corporate income, it may be better to capitalize and amortize the assets over three to five years.

"That's because the owner is entitled to an investment tax credit, which has been increased under the new laws, only if he capitalizes the item," the CPA says. "Combining this with the present value of the depreciation deduction may turn out to be more cost efficient than expensing the purchase in the first year. The trade-off is between receiving the investment tax credit if the item is capitalized and getting a faster write-off but no investment tax credit if the item is expensed."

- Depreciating Non-Residential Real Estate.

Under the accelerated cost recovery system (ACRS), business owners acquiring non-residential real property may elect to use either the accelerated depreciation or the straight-line methods.

Although ACRS allows for a faster write-off, it may not be best. The deductions taken under it are recaptured as ordinary income once the property is sold. For this reason, the investors are advised to elect the straight-line method, unless they have a high ATROR or plan to keep the property for a substantial period of time.

Financial advisers can help business owners determine the precise threshold at which it pays to take advantage of the new tax laws or to opt for the traditional approach.

4

How to Minimize Estimated Taxes

IN the game of give-and-take known as estimated taxes, the shrewdest players strike a delicate balance between penalty avoidance and cash conservation. They pay just enough to stay within the law but not quite enough to cover their full debt to Uncle Sam.

The premise behind this strategy is to save now, pay later. Every dollar of estimated taxes postponed to a later date generates incremental interest or dividends, effectively offsetting part of the tax burden. By basing payments on legal loopholes, small-business owners can reduce their corporation's estimated taxes.

Under ordinary circumstances, federal law requires that estimated payments—made on a quarterly basis—total at least 90 percent of a corporation's actual current tax liability. Should the payments fall below this, a penalty is applied to the underpayment.

"But there are ways around this," says a partner with Seidman & Seidman, CPAs, "ways corporations can base the 90 percent requirement on sums smaller than the firm's current tax liability, thus enabling management to hold on to its money for extended periods of time.

"Assume, for example, that a corporation paid 1983 taxes of $50,000 and that the owner knows that 1984 will be a much more prosperous year, raising his firm's projected tax bill to $100,000. Rather than making current estimated payments of $90,000—which is calculated by taking 90 percent of the projected $100,000 taxes—he can use an alternate approach.

"The law allows for small corporations to base estimated taxes on the full amount of the prior year's tax liability. So in this case, management can pay $50,000 in estimate taxes, thus retaining $50,000 until the full tax is due two and one half months after the fiscal year. In the meantime, the money can be kept in interest-bearing accounts."

This approach, which is allowable only if the corporation paid taxes in the previous year, is a boon for small-growth companies. Because management can continue to peg estimated taxes to prior earnings, it can defer a portion of its tax bill for as long as net profit continues to rise.

CPAs offer the following additional strategies for making estimated payments:

• Companies with heavy seasonal business can base tax payments on "annualized income," computed by projecting yearly earnings on the basis of quarterly results.

"Suppose a calendar-year corporation has net taxable income for the first three months of $20,000," the CPA explains. "From this, management could project an annual income of $80,000 and could link estimated payments to this figure. This in spite of the fact that management knows it will have an especially profitable May, with anticipated income of $60,000 for that month alone. This gain does not have to be figured into the estimated payments until the annualized income is revised later in the year. This allows companies to design estimated payment schedules that take advantage of certain seasonal variances, once again retaining corporate funds for longer periods."

    • One related strategy is to defer income from one taxable year to the next. In many cases, corporations may be advised to structure transactions to allow for realization of income in January rather than the preceding December. Because this reduces the company's tax liability for the prior year, it also reduces the base on which estimated payments may be computed.

Corporations overpaying estimated taxes by $500 or more can receive refunds within forty-five days of the end of the tax year. To qualify for this, the overpayment must be at least 10 percent of the revised tax liability.

5

Tax Savings: It's All in the Accounting

IMAGINE two small companies with equal sales and expenses but one pays less tax than the other. How can that be? It's all in the accounting. Selecting the right accounting method can slash a company's current tax bill.

The fundamental choice is between the accrual and cash methods. Companies with inventories are generally limited to the former. They must record income when earned and expenses when payable. Although this may accurately reflect the state of the business, it is inflexible and allows little opportunity for tax planning.

With the cash method, the corporation records income when received and expenses when paid regardless of when the money was earned or when it was payable. To defer part of its tax bill from one year to the next, the company can postpone year-end billings and accelerate the payment of expenses. This produces lower income and lower current taxes.

"As long as the company keeps growing it can keep on doing this every year and gain what is more or less a permanent deferral," says a manager with Deloitte Haskins & Sells, CPAs. "It only catches up with the firm if it stops growing or is liquidated. The deferral can be substantial. Take a business in the top tax bracket. By postponing $100,000 of income, it can defer as much as $46,000 in federal income taxes.

"So in most cases, where management has the choice, it should opt for the cash method. This is generally open to service firms, including professional practices, but many other types of corporations can qualify, sometimes using a hybrid of both cash and accrual accounting."

Lesser-known accounting methods can also be a boon to small-company finances. Consider the following:

• Installment method accounting can be used by companies selling goods on the installment plan. The benefit is that taxable income is spread over the years as collections are actually made. This reflects the fact that installment sellers recognize gross profit only as it is received, not when a sale is made.

For example, if a merchant sells a $100 chair for which he paid $50, the gross profit is $50. Of a first installment of $30, only 50 percent is considered profit. So the company pays taxes on only $15. Eventually, taxes are paid on the full profit, but this can be spread over several years.

• Percentage-of-completion method can be used by construction companies engaged in long-term projects of more than a year. With this approach, income is reported at various intervals based on the ratio of work completed to the total contract price. Certain operating costs are also deductible as the work progresses.

In contrast, by using the completed contract method, profit on the long-term contract is not reported until the contract is completed and accepted. Even if the company receives progress payments all along, it does not have to recognize profit until the job is done.

"Here again, the company can defer taxes for quite some time," the CPA adds. "This aids cash flow and gives the firm longer use of the money for operating needs or investments. Although recent tax measures have tightened the rules governing the completed contract method, it is still a valid and beneficial approach."

Entrepreneurs first starting out in business can generally choose any recognized accounting method without prior approval from the Internal Revenue Service. They simply have to meet the established guidelines. But companies seeking to change accounting methods must first obtain authorization from the IRS. This is done by filing a form within the first 180 days of the fiscal year in which the new method is to be used. Management must show a valid business reason for the change.

Work with an accountant in selecting the ideal accounting method and in applying it to your business operations.

6

Bad Debts May Have Silver Lining

WHEN is a bad debt not as bad as it seems? When it can reduce the creditor's taxes up to 50 cents on the dollar. Deducting bad debts makes Uncle Sam—always a partner in profits—share in the losses as well.

That's good news for the self-employed. Small-business owners are often stuck with two kinds of bad debts: commercial and personal IOUs. The difference is more than semantics. Just how the Internal Revenue Service treats the loss depends on how it was incurred.

"Because small-business people are often lending money to customers, employees, friends, and relatives, they may have various kinds of loans outstanding at any given time," says a tax manager with the small-business division of Deloitte Haskins & Sells, CPAs. "Their relationship to the borrowers may not matter until and if the loans go bad. At that point, they'll want to establish which were business and which were personal loans because the former can yield more generous tax deductions.

"Put simply, business debts are those that are closely related to a commercial activity. All others are considered non-business debts. Here's the crucial distinction: while business bad debts are fully deductible from gross income, uncollectible non-business debts are treated as short-term capital losses subject to a $3,000 annual deduction limitation with certain carryover rights."

Many taxpayers fail to report bad-debt losses or to establish them as business-related. This can be a costly omission. Consider the following examples:

• To help a customer through a cash crisis, a wholesaler makes what he thinks will be a short-term $10,000 loan. But the borrower goes bankrupt and the IOU isn't worth the paper it's written on. Using the "specific charge-off method," the wholesaler deducts the business bad debt, writing it off in full as it becomes worthless. For a corporation in the top tax bracket, the $10,000 bad debt generates a federal tax saving of $4,600, thus cutting the loss nearly in half.

• A doctor makes $10,000 in personal loans to his patient and all of the debt becomes uncollectible. Because the physician is not in the business of lending money and the loans are not closely related to his professional activities, the bad debts are treated as non-business losses. This means the doctor's write-off in the year of the loss is limited to the portion of the loans he can offset with capital gains plus an additional $3,000 against ordinary income. If he had no capital gains in the year of the loss, his current federal deduction could not exceed $3,000. This reduces the $10,000 loss by a maximum of $1,500. The balance of the loss could, however, be carried over to future years with the same limitations applying.

"Both types of write-offs enable the creditor to turn what may have seemed like a total loss into something not quite so drastic," the tax manager adds. "Taxpayers holding worthless debts should certainly determine if they can be written off and should then take the approach that yields the greatest tax benefits."

For corporations this may mean establishing a reserve for bad debts based on the company's historical loss rate. This allows for accelerated write-offs, taken before the losses actually occur.

A company with average annual debt losses of $50,000 on a $500,000 average receivables balance has a 10 percent loss rate. Should its receivables balance increase to $700,000, it can add to its reserve and deduct an additional $20,000. Management does not have to wait until this increment of bad debt is declared worthless.

Work with an accountant or a tax attorney in structuring bad debt deductions and reserves.

7

Accounting Change Can Slash Taxes

T HERE'S more to inventory management than simply keeping track of parts and products. Just how small business accounts for its inventories can have a dramatic impact on the bottom line. A timely change in accounting procedures can save thousands of tax dollars annually.

In periods of rising costs, companies may profit by switching from the standard FIFO (first-in, first-out) method of accounting to the LIFO (last-in, first-out) alternative. This applies the most recent, higher cost of goods to current revenues, thus reducing the stated profit and the resulting tax.

Arthur Andersen & Co., the national accounting firm, gives the following example:

Assume that at the beginning of the year, ABC Co. has 500 widgets on hand for which it paid $10 each ($5,000). Months later, it purchases an additional 500 widgets for $20 each ($10,000). Its annual sales are 500 widgets at $25 each ($12,500).

With FIFO, it would figure taxable profit as revenue ($12,500) minus the cost of first-in goods ($5,000) for a net of $7,500. Under LIFO, the computation is $12,500 minus the $10,000 cost of last-in goods for a taxable net of $2,500. Nothing changes except the way the company reports its income and the amount of taxes it pays. In this case, $5,000 is shielded from taxes.

"LIFO works best when prices are on the rise," says an Arthur Andersen partner. "By charging higher costs to revenues, it partially insulates companies from the ravages of inflation. I think some firms can benefit more from this simple accounting change than from anything found in the major tax reform laws of recent years."

Adds a partner with Main Hurdman, CPAs: "One of the great attractions of LIFO is that companies can wait to make the election until they file their tax returns. This gives them the benefit of hindsight. They can look back to see if prices rose enough during the year to make the change worthwhile. If inventory costs fell during the period, the change to LIFO is probably not a good idea."

The president of a manufacturer of hospital and home care medical equipment says that his firm saved $125,000 in taxes the first year it converted to LIFO. "We made the move as a cash-flow maneuver and we have been very pleased with the results. I believe that management's job is to conserve cash rather than to inflate profit, and LIFO works toward cash conservation. Although there is some extra work involved with LIFO accounting, it's well worth the effort."

Internal Revenue Service rulings have made LIFO elections even more attractive to small business:

• Many companies can now report LIFO profits for tax purposes and FIFO profits to investors or creditors. The business owner/manager reporting $25,000 in profits to the IRS can use supplemental information to show a banker that profit would have been $50,000 under FIFO. Evidence of the higher figure may be crucial to obtaining the loan.

• Beginning with the tax year 1982, companies can use simplified computation rules for LIFO reporting.

Still, there are drawbacks to making LIFO elections:

• LIFO may have a negative impact in periods of sustained deflation. The company will have to apply its lowest costs to revenues, thus increasing taxable earnings.

• Once the LIFO election is made, IRS approval is required to return to FIFO.

Management should explore the pros and cons of LIFO elections with an accountant or tax attorney.

8

Take More Depreciation, Save on Taxes

JUST how a small business depreciates its assets can have a major impact on its tax bill. By hunting for little-known sources of depreciation, management can take additional deductions, adding thousands of dollars to the bottom line.

Put simply, depreciation is an accounting treatment of an asset's cost over its useful life. Typically, as the asset ages, a percentage of its cost is written off. This deduction is taken for a specified number of years until, theoretically, the asset has no value. Internal Revenue formulas specify how the depreciation is to be structured.

Although depreciation does not produce cash, it saves money by cutting taxes. For companies in the 50 percent bracket, every dollar of depreciation saves 50 cents that would otherwise go to Uncle Sam.

"Although most small companies are familiar with the major types of depreciation, they often miss out on the obscure items," says a tax partner with the national accounting firm of Main Hurdman. "When I show my clients that they can actually depreciate something like spare parts, they say, 'Fantastic—you just saved me a lot of money!'"

CPAs suggest the following money-saving strategies:

• Depreciate spare machinery parts. The general rule is that equipment cannot be depreciated until it is put into service. But spare parts for an existing machine can be depreciated as components of the total cost of the machine even if they are not installed in the operating equipment until a later date. Because small companies are unaware of this distinction, they lose out on the deduction.°

• Intangibles such as patents, copyrights, and covenants not to compete are depreciable items with significant legal as well as economic benefits.

"Entrepreneurs buying businesses should demand that the owners sign an agreement not to compete with them," says a Main Hurdman manager. "Without this covenant, the seller may go right back into business as an aggressive competitor. The non-compete clause provides valuable protection.

"As an added benefit, it can also be written off. To do so, a dollar value must be placed on the covenant and it must be included in the sales contract. If so, it can likely be depreciated over the number of years the covenant covers."

• In constructing a building, the land is not depreciable, but excavation, grading, and soil-removal costs

---

°Equipment and/or parts of $5,000 or less may be written off in the year of purchase. This may be preferable to depreciating the item, however it does not allow for claiming the investment tax credit. A comparative analysis must be done.

can be included in the cost of the structure and can be depreciated.

"Too often, such work is considered part of the land and the owner loses the benefit of it until he turns around and sells it," the Main Hurdman partner adds. "But in a carefully constructed transaction, he can get immediate benefits through the write-off."

• Computer software developed in-house is subject to an election whereby a deduction for development costs can be taken immediately or spread out over a sixty-month period.

Work with an accountant to find all depreciable items and to structure the deductions to comply with IRS formulas. Although depreciation guidelines have been simplified in recent years, there are still gray areas and differences between state and federal rules.

9
Gift-Leasebacks Can Cut Taxes

AN intriguing strategy for cutting federal taxes calls for a strange reversal of family roles: turning children into landlords and parents into tenants. The goal is to shift income from high- to low-tax bracket family members.

It works this way. By transferring ownership of business-related property to a trust created for their children, and then leasing the property from the trust, entrepreneurs and professionals can effectively distribute income to their offspring, who are likely subject to a smaller tax bite. The net result is that more money stays in the family, and less goes to Uncle Sam.

"With this so-called gift-leaseback, the rental expense comes out of the parents' taxable income and is converted into income for the lightly taxed children," says a tax manager for Fox & Co., CPAs. "What's more, a transfer is often made when a property is completely depreciated, generating a substantial tax deduction that would not otherwise be available to the parents. The tactic can be used for a wide range of business assets including office buildings, stores and equipment."

The CPA cites the following example. Parents transfer a $90,000 building to a Clifford Trust set up for their two children. According to the terms of the trust, the property will revert to the parents in ten years and one day. (Clifford Trusts must stay in force for more than ten years.) In the meantime, the income from the property—in this case paid by the parents in the form of rent—accumulates in the trust for the benefit of the children. Assuming a rental of $13,500 per year, the gift shifts $135,000 in taxable income to the children over the period of the trust.

"If the parents are in the 50 percent bracket, this will reduce their federal income taxes by $67,500," the CPA adds. "Providing the trustee distributes all income to the children on an equal basis, they will pay taxes of approximately $17,000. The net savings is $50,500.

"Although some people may fear a gift tax when the asset is shifted to the trust, proper tax planning can avoid this. Parents are entitled to make a tax-free gift to a trust of $10,000 for each child. Furthermore, the amount is doubled if both parents make the gift together.

"In the example of the $90,000 building transfer, the parents are entitled to a combined exclusion from gift tax of $40,000. Because Internal Revenue Service tables value the ten-year interest in the building at $39,744, the gift will not be subject to tax. Also, the parents can each presently make additional tax-free gifts of $275,000 during their lifetime and this exemption will increase until it reaches $600,000 in 1987."

But there are caveats.

"The IRS often challenges these transactions on various grounds," says a CPA with the national accounting firm of Price Waterhouse. "But they usually hold up in court appeals, providing the gift-leasebacks are structured so that the trustee is truly independent—here it is best to use a lawyer, banker, or accountant—and that the parents have divested themselves of control of the property until it reverts to them."

Other safeguards include:

- Putting the terms of the lease in writing.
- Setting a fair rental based on comparable market rates.
- Indicating a genuine business purpose for the transaction. When real estate is involved, professional management of the property, through the trustee, may be cited.
- Money from the trust should be used for other than the children's basic support.

"In some cases, economic factors may rule against a gift-leaseback," the Fox & Co. CPA advises. "If the property is financed, the transfer may trigger a 'due on sale' clause which could cause the debt to be refinanced at a higher interest rate. Also, if appreciated property has been refinanced for an amount in excess of its original cost, the transfer to the trust may create a taxable event for the donor. Both factors may wipe out the income-shifting tax benefits."

Explore gift-leasebacks with an accountant or tax attorney.

10
Estate Freezes Can Cut Taxes

E VER think of putting your estate into the deep freeze? It may be the best way for the self-employed to pass business interests to the next generation of family members.

Estate freezing refers to any number of techniques that restructure asset ownership so that virtually all future appreciation benefits children or other heirs. This helps individuals place a ceiling on the value of their estates, thus reducing the tax liability when the assets are transferred.

"If structured properly, estate freezing consistently survives challenges from the Internal Revenue Service," says a tax manager with Seidman & Seidman, CPAs. "Just which freezing technique to use depends on personal circumstances, but small-business owners should make certain that the one they select offers three major benefits.

"They should be able to retain control of the assets for as long as they wish, maintain a desired income level, and minimize or eliminate transfer taxes on future appreciation

by shifting that increase in value to younger family
members."

Consider the following estate freezing strategies:

• Establish a multiclass partnership with two types of
partners, general and preferred. At the creation of the
partnership, the value of the preferred stock is frozen.
Although the preferred partner—usually the founder—has
first rights to liquidation distributions and income up to a
predetermined limit, all appreciation beyond this level goes
to the general partners. This motivates the new generation
to continue the firm's growth pattern while simultaneously
limiting the value of the preferred partner's estate.

• Owners of closely held corporations can achieve
similar results by selling a portion of their common stock to
family members. They then exchange the remaining
common shares for preferred stock equal to the value of the
common stock surrendered.

Because the senior shareholder's interests are tied up in
preferred stock, he forfeits any future growth in the
common stock. This puts a ceiling on the value of the estate.
Further reductions in value can be achieved by making
lifetime gifts of the preferred stock, within the $10,000
annual gift exclusion ($20,000 for joint gifts given by a
taxpayer and spouse).

• Individuals holding stock in publicly traded companies can use personal holding companies (PHCs) to
reduce both current and estate taxes. The shareholder
transfers his stock in the public company to a PHC. By
issuing one or more classes of PHC common and preferred
stock, he can control assets, retain income, minimize
transfer taxes, and freeze his estate.

"When the personal holding company is formed, the
founding shareholder retains all classes of preferred stock,"

the tax manager explains, "and either sells or gives the common stock to his children. Because the PHC's value rests mainly with the preferred stock, the common shares are of nominal worth, thus avoiding gift taxes when transferred. This works much like a preferred stock exchange except that the PHC is used for investment assets and is subject to special rules."

There are drawbacks. All estate freezing techniques are fraught with complex tax law issues, potential IRS challenges, changes in the law and other legal caveats. Small-business owners should review the alternatives and the implications with experienced attorneys and accountants. Make certain that the estate freeze plan you select is appropriate for your circumstances and offers maximum financial advantages.

"Estate freezing always makes sense from a tax standpoint," says a partner with the accounting firm of Deloitte, Haskins & Sells. "But the owner must be psychologically prepared for it. If he continues to expand the business and sees the fruits of that effort going to others, he may be dissatisfied. It is best to hold off on a freeze until the owner is ready to take a less active role in the company."

11

Tax Planning Battles Inflation, Saves Money

SOMETIMES, the worst problems are really opportunities in disguise. Take the dual demons of inflation and taxes. A close look reveals that they are not just double trouble: one can be used to combat the other.

When inflation distorts traditional income patterns, once satisfactory earnings increases are barely enough to keep the self-employed running in place. Rising costs and steeper tax brackets wipe out personal and corporate gains. The growth in revenues is mostly illusory.

"Should a company's shareholders be happy if they see corporate profits increasing by 10 percent?" asks a CPA with the national accounting firm of Price Waterhouse & Co. "Might an individual improve his standard of living with a 10 percent raise? On the surface, yes. But closer inspection shows that in most cases a mere 10 percent jump means that the company or individual is losing ground.

"The corporation may discover that in any given year it is paying 15 percent more to replace inventories, while new plant and equipment cost two or three times what they cost ten years before. The 10 percent boost in profits simply isn't enough. The individual—burdened by the same double-digit inflation—finds that, in addition, his 10 percent raise has pushed him into a higher tax bracket. Purchasing power has slipped away like quicksilver."

Although the problem seems insurmountable, it is not. The seeds to the solution can be found in the tax system itself. Wise tax planning can help to preserve capital and generally to mitigate the ravages of inflation. Experts recommend the following strategies:

• Explore the last-in, first-out (LIFO) method of inventory accounting. During periods of inflation, this helps to reduce the small firm's tax burden, thus making more money available for obtaining replacement inventory. LIFO allows for the most recent, and probably most expensive, inventory purchases of the taxable period to be charged to the cost of sales. It provides a more accurate reflection of the costs of carrying inventory in times of rising prices.

• Set up a reserve for bad debts. Rather than deducting worthless debts one by one, a company can set up and deduct a reserve against bad debts. As accounts receivable increase, the size of the reserve may grow. Although the initial reserve set up in the year of the adoption must be deducted within ten years, the reserve method provides a permanent "float" of bad debt deductions.

"One should keep in mind however that in order to avoid problems with the Internal Revenue Service, a company using the reserve method must be vigilant in writing off worthless accounts," the CPA adds. "This is because previous years' write-offs are used by the IRS to determine the current allowable addition to the reserve."

• Seek ways to maximize depreciation. Techniques for highly accelerated depreciation can cut taxes immediately and provide continuing benefits when the company buys new assets each year.

Some depreciation strategies are not well known. When purchasing or constructing a building, for example, component depreciation may be a wise course. With this approach, each major component of the facility is depreciated separately. This can result in bigger initial write-offs because components such as roofing and heating may have shorter lives than the building shell.

• Establish Employee Stock Ownership Plans (ESOPs). A simple stock bonus plan enables a company to net tax deductions without making cash outlays. Through this technique, employees are awarded bonuses with shares of company stock. The firm deducts its contribution to the ESOP, workers have a stake in the firm, and management preserves its cash.

All tax strategies, regardless of their merits, must be viewed in the context of a company's entire operations. Every tax-planning option carries drawbacks, caveats, and potential conflicts with the IRS. It is important to review carefully all plans with tax professionals before implementing them. In most cases, more sophisticated tax procedures generate higher professional fees. The ultimate savings can, however, make this a sound investment in long-term fiscal health and prosperity.

12

Trade Tax Benefits, Cut Equipment Costs

S MALL companies in the market for business equipment can cut financing costs by trading the tax benefits that go with asset ownership. Tax-wise leasing deals let management separate the wheat from the chaff: they gain use of the asset but turn the intangibles into cash.

The major distinction between buying and leasing business equipment is that buyers gain two key tax benefits—depreciation and the investment tax credit—that can reduce the cost of the purchase by cutting taxes on the company's profits. Because this tax break is generally unavailable to lessees—who simply rent assets rather than own them—many companies shy away from leasing. They view it as a costly alternative to a standard purchase.

"But some companies cannot use the tax benefits of ownership," says a tax partner with Price Waterhouse, CPAs. "Start-up ventures still in the red and established firms with a substantial amount of deductions from other sources cannot make current use of the equipment depreciation or tax credit. These companies may not have any profits to shelter. Leasing has always been a way for such firms to transfer tax benefits to other corporations in exchange for lower financing rates."

Although Congress and the Internal Revenue Service have tightened the rules on some of the most popular tax-oriented leasing deals, leasing can still be used to cut equipment financing costs.

In a so-called true lease arrangement, the small company works with a leasing company in placing an equipment order.

"Assume ABC Company decides to automate and orders $100,000 worth of production equipment," says a leasing company president. "At this time, ABC's accountant makes management aware that the firm cannot make current use of ownership tax benefits. Rather than letting those tax benefits go to waste, ABC can assign the equipment order to a leasing company. ABC will still take delivery of the equipment but it will be owned by the lessor.

"ABC gains because the leasing company grants it an advantageous financing rate in exchange for the tax benefits it has passed to the lessor. For example, if we were doing a straight finance deal without getting tax benefits, we might base the payments on a 14 percent interest rate. But when we pick up the ownership tax breaks, we can reduce the underlying rate to as low as 8 percent for a lessee with a good credit standing. We make money on the tax benefits and can pass the savings on to the lessee in the form of lower financing costs."

The financial vice-president of a toiletry firm agrees. "We have found that leasing with the investment tax credit pass-through saves us substantially over other forms of financing. Before leasing our IBM System 38, we explored

various options, and leasing turned out to be the most
advantageous. That's because we have tax credits from
other equipment acquisitions and can't make use of the
additional benefits at this time."

At the end of the lease period, the equipment may be
sold to the lessee for its fair market value. The lessee may
keep it, trade it in for a new model, or sell it.

Before leasing or buying business assets, it is always
best to shop the market for the best financing rates.
Compare the terms offered by banks, finance companies,
lessors, and manufacturers.

"Leasing is just another form of financing," says a
managing director for Lehman Brothers Kuhn Loeb,
investment bankers. "As with all other capital-raising
techniques, it is important to scan the market for all
available options. Sometimes—especially when the company doesn't need current tax deductions—leasing may be
the wise choice. At other times, it may be better to buy."

Work with a financial adviser in making and implementing buy/lease decisions.

13

PAYSOPs Make It Pay to Give Company Stock

G IVING employees a piece of the business has always been the best way to raise morale and boost productivity. Now it can also cut thousands of dollars from the company's tax bill.

This three-for-one return comes with the introduction of PAYSOPs, a type of qualified benefit plan. Created by a provision of the Economic Recovery Tax Act, PAYSOPs enable management to fund employee plans with shares of company stock and to receive a dollar for dollar tax credit for the contribution.

"The PAYSOP is a welcome to both employers and employees that will allow greater numbers of employees to participate in the ownership of their companies," says a vice-president of Towers, Perrin, Forster & Crosby, a consulting firm specializing in benefit plans. "It is likely to become a popular form of employee benefit once its advantages are recognized more widely."

PAYSOPs work like this. Management establishes a qualified plan and on an annual basis contributes to it cash or shares of the company's stock to a maximum of one half percent of participating employees' compensation. (This increases to three quarters of a percent in 1987.) If the contribution is made in cash, the plan's trustee has thirty days from the tax filing date to purchase stock with the proceeds. The company stock used to fund the plan need not be publicly traded but must carry certain minimum voting and dividend rights.

"Contributions made under the PAYSOP are normally allocated on the basis of what each participant's compensation bears to the total compensation of the employees participating in the plan," explains a partner active in small-business services for Price Waterhouse, CPAs. "In computing this ratio, no compensation in excess of $100,000 for any participant is considered.

"The plan must provide for full and immediate vesting. It may not provide for any distributions within seven years of the date on which the compensation was allocated to the participant's account, except in the case of death, disability, separation from service, or pursuant to certain corporate reorganizations."

The following are additional PAYSOP provisions:

• Contributions must be made no later than thirty days after the company's tax filing date, including extensions.

• Tax credit is claimed by attaching a statement to the tax return. The credit is limited to the first $25,000 of corporate tax liability plus 90 percent of the excess tax liability over $25,000.

"The real beauty of PAYSOPs, as far as small business is concerned, is that they allow for the tax credit to be based on payroll," says a Towers, Perrin executive. "Before this, with so-called TRASOPs, the credit was based on the amount of a company's capital investment. Because few small firms make large capital investments, TRASOPs did not serve their needs.

"I recommend serious consideration of PAYSOPs not only because of the tax credits but also because sharing ownership in a company is still one of the best ways to motivate employees."

But there are drawbacks. Management must grant certain voting rights and must disclose proxy information that it may prefer to keep confidential. What's more, if the company is not making money, there may be no need for tax credits.

The best approach is to work with professionals in weighing PAYSOPs' pros and cons and in structuring the plans to meet company objectives and legal requirements.

14
How to Fight the IRS

S MALL companies slapped with unfair tax bills have two choices: turn the other cheek or fight back. Sometimes, the aggressive approach pays off, as just the threat of court action can win substantial concessions.

Tax experts claim that many small firms and their owners are hesitant about appealing an Internal Revenue Service call for additional taxes. This timidity can be costly. A recent IRS *Commissioner's Annual Report* reveals that taxpayers committed to court action often win settlements in their favor.

Taxpayers dissatisfied with the way the IRS district office is handling their case can seek an appellate conference at the regional level. This is often a first step on the road to court. If the IRS knows that the taxpayer is determined to take legal action, it is likely to make concessions rather than risk the uncertainties of a court case.

"Sometimes, the best strategy is to file a petition with the U.S. Tax Court, an independent body not part of the IRS," says a tax manager with Siegel & Mendlowitz, CPAs. "This shifts the case from an agent, who is assigned to search for every opportunity for additional taxes, to an IRS attorney, whose primary interest is to dispose of cases before they come to trial. The attorneys are inclined to work out mutually agreeable settlements.

Adds an IRS spokesman: "Our appeal attorneys do bring another dimension to the cases they review. While agents look mostly at established rules and regulations, the attorneys must consider the hazards of litigation. They must be aware that we can lose the case in court. With this in mind, the IRS gives them more leeway in resolving taxpayer disputes."

Taxpayers may want to go to court should negotiations with the IRS fail to produce satisfactory results. Accountants and attorneys offer the following guidelines:

• "Go to Tax Court only when the IRS refuses to compromise in the appeals process," says one lawyer/ CPA. "In court, you risk losing the case as well as having to pay attorneys' fees. What's more, Tax Court cases can take three years to come to trial. If the taxpayer loses, he'll have to pay interest computed from the date the taxes were originally due. This can add substantially to his tax bill."

• Be aware that the IRS is more likely to compromise on facts rather than interpretations of the law. For example, while IRS officials may agree to a certain questionable deduction in a specific case, they may not authorize a whole category of controversial deductions.

• Taxpayers have a good chance of achieving favorable settlements in matters where recent court decisions have countered IRS rules. Be aggressive here. In most cases, the IRS will bend backward to keep this issue from going to court again.

• "Be prepared to go to court for cases involving tax shelters, especially if your deductions are based on estimated valuations of property, such as buildings," the tax manager adds. "While the IRS tends to interpret these issues strictly, the courts may take a more liberal view."

• Consider all the avenues of legal appeal including District Court, Court of Claims, and the U.S. Tax Court's small case division. The latter hears cases involving sums of less than $5,000. Here, procedures are simplified and taxpayers may feel more comfortable in handling the matter without an attorney.

Work with a professional in planning tax case appeals.

15

How to Audit Your CPAs

JUST as your accountants are closing the books on another tax year, the time may be right to launch an audit of your own. Turn the tables on the CPAs, checking them for bottom line performance and commitment to your account. A periodic review of financial services helps small companies attract and retain the highest caliber professionals.

Typically, once an accounting firm is hired, management is loathe to replace it. As the CPAs become familiar with the company's bookkeeping system and privy to its most confidential information, they assume a privileged status that insulates them from objective review. But small-business owners must challenge this by subjecting the practitioners to a layman's audit.

Use the following checklist to review your CPAs' performance:

- Do the practitioners engage in "creative accounting"?

Even the smallest firms can benefit from accounting services that go beyond bookkeeping to sophisticated tax-cutting strategies. While uninspired CPAs will view a business owner's family as mere dependents, creative accountants seize opportunities for income splitting and tax reduction. Although a layman is not in position to judge the wisdom of an accountant's professional practices, one good sign of creativity is the introduction of new ideas and financial procedures. Does the CPA regularly recommend new ways of doing things? Do you see concrete evidence of business savings or personal tax savings? Even if the business has few tax-cutting opportunities, the message often comes through that the accountant is trying.

"For the first twenty-three years of running my own business, I used the same accounting firm," says the president of a family-owned distributorship. "Because we never had major disagreements, and because there was no trouble with the IRS, I believed everything should be left alone. But when I hired a consultant to review all aspects of our business, he found that we were losing out on dozens of tax-saving opportunities. At his suggestion, we hired a new CPA firm that, for the same fees, has set in motion a number of excellent programs. They've switched our cash reserves from a standard money market fund to a qualified dividend plan that's virtually tax free to corporations, and they've established an attractive pension plan that lets us salt away more than $40,000 a year in deductible contributions."

• Does the CPA meet with management on a regular basis?

As a firm prospers, expands, or even contracts in response to a slumping market, the repercussions affect everything from estimated taxes to cash flow. To compensate for this, the CPA must make financial adjustments across-the-board. But this is not possible if the accountant restricts his visits to tax season only. This lack of continuity in the accountant-client relationship rules against sound tax planning. Although more frequent contact may generate higher fees, the small-business owner should insist on a minimum schedule of monthly meetings.

• Does the client's billing reflect the caliber of professionals handling the account?

Accounting firms generally charge for their services on an hourly basis, the precise rate depending on the stature of the practitioner performing the work. In a typical case, fees may range from $100 per hour for a senior partner to $40 per hour for the youngest member of the firm. Because a vast gulf of experience and expertise separates the two, paying the higher fee may be a good idea when the work involves sophisticated procedures but it can be overkill for simple assignments such as tending to a general ledger.

• Are the accountants experienced in the client's type of business?

This industry specialization can be a key factor in cementing a productive client-accountant relationship. CPA firms with specialized practices often have sophisticated computer programs designed to perform complex transactions common to the industry with unusual speed and accuracy.

The selection of an accounting firm can never be based on a single criterion. Trust, loyalty, and rapport are as important as professional considerations. The best approach is to review the firm's performance on a regular basis. Should your audit reveal a glaring weakness, give the firm the opportunity to correct it. At the same time, feel free to ask other CPA firms for a free consultation. Work with the accountants that offer the best mix of skills and services.

II

RAISING MONEY

16

How Investment Bankers Can Help Small Business

WHEN a West Coast–based developer of retirement communities found itself burdened by skyrocketing interest costs that had climbed above the record prime rate to 28 percent, management searched for a way to replace its debt with a less-volatile source of capital. The ultimate solution, simple but ingenious, was to sell convertible debentures, to repay the banks from the proceeds and thus to shift the corporation's obligation to fixed instruments that carried interest rates of less than half the bank's highest charges.

This fiscal miracle of sorts was performed not by the company's management, its accountants, or its attorneys. Instead, credit goes to the peerless specialists in corporate finance: investment bankers.

"We were called in to review the corporation's debt problems with an eye toward recommending a viable alternative to its heavy bank borrowing," says Stephen S. Weisglass, president of Ladenburg, Thalmann & Co., Inc., a small, by Wall Street standards, New York investment banking house.

"After a review of the corporation's finances, we decided that the convertible debenture approach offered the ideal mix of fixed-rate financing and potential equity participation. The $27.5 million worth of fifteen-year, 12.5 percent debentures assured the corporation of a stable interest rate, which is important to sound management, and offered the prospect—thanks to the convertible feature—of turning the debt into equity."

Ladenburg's shrewd restructuring of the company's debt is indicative of the key role an investment banking firm can play in a corporation's financial affairs. It also illustrates that investment banking services are not restricted to the huge multinational corporations. Even the smallest businesses can afford and benefit from investment banking relationships.

The problem is, most entrepreneurs think of investment bankers only in terms of the venerable Wall Street giants— Goldman Sachs, Lehman Brothers, Morgan Stanley—that are closely aligned with the Fortune 1000. Because these firms specialize in enormous transactions of $100 million to more than $1 billion each, they are ill suited for the relatively modest capital requirements of small and mid-size firms. But a second tier of investment banks, those specializing in emerging ventures, are willing to handle deals their more illustrious colleagues generally decline.

"Firms like ours are willing to do for small business what the Merill Lynches and the First Bostons do for huge corporations," Weisglass adds. "We've managed or co-managed forty-five public offerings for small firms, some of which were start-ups. In deciding to work with a company, we consider size to be of less importance than potential. If we think the latter is there, we'll often find a way to work with them."

A spokesman for the Securities Industry Association, a trade group representing many prominent investment banking firms, says, "The relationship with an investment banker can begin quite early in a company's growth cycle. Ideally, the contact is made before the young firm depletes its initial bank loan or seed capital. If the investment bankers are involved from the start, they are in exceptionally good position to help arrange the additional financing that will be necessary to fuel the firm's expansion."

Typically, investment bankers are introduced to prospective clients through accountants, consultants, and commercial bankers. "Once the initial contact is made, the investment bankers visit your place of business, taking a crash course in your company—what makes it tick," says the executive vice-president of a small home-furnishings concern. "They have an awesome facility for identifying your hidden strengths and weaknesses and for recommending strategies that use the former to correct the latter. In the three years we've been working with investment bankers, they've provided us with three widely different services, each of which had a favorable impact on our financial performance. People tend to think of investment bankers solely in terms of going public, but they have much more to offer."

Major investment banking services include:

• Merger and acquisition departments serve as marriage brokers for two or more companies. They find the parties for the union, determine the firms' market values, and recommend how they should unite. Active bankers maintain files of entrepreneurs who are looking to buy, sell, or merge. By successfully merging a small business into a substantially larger corporation, the banker can help to assure the firm of a steady flow of capital for its future growth and can enable the principals to exchange all or part of their stock for cash.

• Money management activities range from administering corporate pension plans to supervising business owners' personal investments. Related to this, the banks often serve as syndicators of tax-sheltered investment programs. Because they are close to the money centers and are expert at financial analysis, investment bankers often chalk up exceptional results in stock and bond recommendations.

• Public offerings seek to raise equity capital through the sale of stock to outside investors. This can be an initial public offering (for ventures that were privately owned) or a secondary offering (for public companies seeking additional rounds of financing).

"A public offering can be structured to benefit both the company and its principals," Weisglass explains. "In an offering we managed for a perfume distributor, we raised approximately $12.2 million. Of that, about $5.5 million went to the company and $5.7 million to the principals, who sold some of their own shares to the public. The real beauty is that the company gained capital, and the principals, who still retained 59 percent of the company after the offering, got liquid after many years of having all of their interests tied up in stock.

• Private placements secure business financing through negotiation with financial institutions, including insurance companies and pension funds.

"Traditionally, we seek private placements when a company is in the earliest stages of its life cycle and is not quite ready for a public offering," says a vice-president of the Illinois Co., Chicago-based investment bankers. "In exchange for some form of debt plus an equity kicker, the financing institution will take on the high-risk commitments that commercial banks refuse to accept. Private placement for small business typically ranges from $500,000 and up."

Although investment bankers are generally hired on a project basis, with the fees for small accounts ranging from 5 percent to 10 percent of the money raised, they can serve in an ongoing capacity as members of a firm's board of directors.

"An investment banker on the board can provide management advice, monitor financial performance, move quickly if money is needed, and act as an objective intermediary between the company and its major share-holders," the Illinois Co. executive explains.

Two key factors should be considered when selecting the right investment banker for special projects or consulting relationships:

• Look for a bank that is big enough to wield some weight in the capital markets but not so big as to focus its efforts exclusively on huge corporate accounts. Check out the bank's track record. Does it have a history of service to modest-sized firms? Seek references from accountants as well as from the bank's current and former clients.

• Favor the bank that has the most experience in your field. This industry specialization can indicate that the bankers are familiar with your company's special needs. "One of our clients was able to sell, for a substantial figure, a division that had been losing money," says a CPA active with small-business accounts. "In spite of the losses, the division had value because of its underlying assets. But it took an investment banker with experience in the company's field to see that value and to find a buyer willing to pay for it."

A list of the Securities Industry Association's member firms may be obtained by writing the organization at 120 Broadway, New York, NY 10271. This may be a good starting point for launching a review of investment banking firms. Experts suggest meeting with at least three firms before committing to a relationship.

17

Rule Makes Raising Money Easier

GOODBYE red tape. A ruling by the Securities and Exchange Commission has paved the way for small companies to raise money through private offerings without wading through piles of paperwork and putting up with endless delays. They go straight to investors and take home the cash.

It is all made possible by Regulation D offerings, a simplified mechanism for raising capital. Companies seeking up to $500,000 can now sell equity and debt issues, limited partnership interests in oil and gas ventures, and virtually any type of security to an unlimited number of investors without prior registration. They must simply file a brief statistical report with the SEC within fifteen days of the first securities sale.

When larger sums are required, public or closely held companies can raise up to $5 million by selling unregistered securities to a maximum of thirty-five investors plus an unlimited number of "accredited investors." Accredited investors are defined as banks, insurance and investment companies, pension plans and tax-exempt organizations, directors and officers of the companies raising the capital, parties investing a minimum of $150,000 in the deal, and individuals with net worth of $1 million or annual income of at least $200,000 over the past three years.

"There's no doubt that Regulation D is a blessing for small business," says an SEC specialist with the national accounting firm of Main Hurdman. "It saves them time and money and goes a long way toward seeing they get the capital they need to grow over the years. In the past, when a full registration had to be approved by the SEC before the financing could proceed, companies had to spend $100,000 or more in registration fees just to raise $1 million. Now they need not spend more than a few thousand dollars for the services of a securities attorney and perhaps some accounting work."

One company in the computer memory field credits its founding to Regulation D. "We believed we had the technology to produce superior computer disc packs and disc cartridges," says a company vice-president, "but we needed seed money to get the company off the ground. Through the mechanism of Regulation D, we raised more than $1 million. We sold securities to three major investors and to a venture capital firm. Our company is now on its way, in part, because Regulation D did precisely what it is supposed to do. It cut out the red tape and made raising money for a promising company quite easy."

One drawback to Regulation D offerings is that investors may have to hold the securities for at least two years. Those who favor quick trades or who reject highly speculative issues are likely to shy away from Regulation D securities. Small companies could go bankrupt before the investors are allowed to sell their interests.

"But there are advantages to these investments as well. "Most companies making Regulation D offerings are privately held. If the corporations eventually go public, the original investors stand to profit handsomely. Small firms must find investors who will accept risk in return for the chance to net big capital gains."

One caveat is that state and federal securities laws are not uniform and in certain cases state guidelines can offset some of the benefits of Regulation D. Companies holding any type of securities sales must make certain that they conform with state laws wherever the issues are sold. This means working closely with securities attorneys throughout the offering process.

18

How to Fund High-Risk Ventures

T HE most productive relationships in American business team high-technology companies with speculative investors. The two are made for each other. Investors have the capital; creative companies have the know-how to make it grow. Add a dash of tax benefits and you have the next Xerox in the making.

That's the dream behind the formation of research and development limited partnerships. Increasingly popular in the small-business community, these investment vehicles provide entrepreneurs with high-risk capital while simultaneously serving as a tax shelter for high-bracket investors. In a period of volatile interest rates and tight-fisted bank lending, this may be the best way to finance the development of new products, systems, and services.

"High interest rates have enhanced the appeal of R&D ventures for those companies requiring capital for ongoing research and development," says a partner with Price Waterhouse, CPAs. "And the tax benefits associated with these ventures make them attractive investment opportunities.

"Typically, capital to fund the research and development is contributed by investors in exchange for limited partnership interests. R&D expenses are deductible by the partnership, and royalty income from successful efforts may be treated as capital gain. Structuring an R&D venture as a limited partnership allows investors to realize a significant accelerated tax savings, while enjoying the protection of limited liability."

Put simply, the R&D ventures work like this: ABC Co. needs capital to engage in research and development aimed at producing a new product or service. Management cannot obtain bank financing or rejects the high interest rates quoted by traditional lenders. To get around this, the firm contracts with a group of investors to finance the research and development in exchange for title to the product or patent.

The investors, joined together in a limited partnership, are willing to take the risk because they can immediately[*] deduct the R&D expenses as tax losses, thus offsetting taxes on other sources of income.

"If the plan calls for investors to contribute $100,000 each, they can take this entire write-off in the year of the contribution,"[*] says a partner with Arthur Young, CPAs. "So the deduction will effectively reduce the out-of-pocket investment, assuming the investors are in the 50 percent bracket, to half the total paid out or $50,000."

But tax benefits are only part of the equation. "On a long-term basis, the venture hopes that the R&D will result in one or more products or processes which can be

[*]Providing the actual research is conducted within the year of the deduction or within 8½ months of the following year.

exploited commercially," the tax expert explains. "Rather than manufacture and market the product itself, the partnership often grants an option to license or purchase the technology resulting from the R&D to the entity performing the R&D, namely the entrepreneur or small business. Upon exercise of the option, the partnership will be entitled to royalties based on the revenues produced by the product or process. If structured properly, such royalty income can be treated as long-term capital gain to the partners."

If all goes according to plan, ABC Co. winds up with the rights to manufacture and market the technology it produced. In return, it pays royalties to the investors who risked their capital to fund the research and development. That's the beauty of the plan: the small company gains the cash and the resources to compete in the marketplace and the investors gain an attractive mix of tax deductions and potential capital gains.

Attorneys, accountants, and investment bankers can help creative companies attract limited partners for R&D ventures. Because these financing vehicles are fraught with complex legal and accounting issues, it is important to have them planned by professionals experienced in the field.

19

Subchapter S Law May Save You Money

A LAW liberalizing the rules for Subchapter S corporations can bring substantial tax savings to four of every five privately owned companies. That's the opinion of prominent CPAs specializing in small-business practice.

"The Subchapter S Revision Tax Act can be a shot in the arm to small business," says a tax partner for Ernst & Whinney, the national accounting firm. "Subchapter S permits a closely held corporation to be taxed at the shareholder level, thus avoiding corporate federal income taxes. Because the act has improved many of the finer points of Subchapter S status, many more corporations will want to make Subchapter S elections, and many partnerships and proprietorships will want to incorporate to take advantage of the new benefits."

Consider the act's major provisions:

• Subchapter S corporations may now have a maximum of thirty-five shareholders, up from the previous ceiling of twenty-five.

"This makes it possible to attract more investors to the corporation," says a partner with Seidman & Seidman, CPAs. "Many investors like to work through the Subchapter S organization because they can report earnings and losses on personal tax returns and still have the protection of limited liability."

• Transfer of stock ownership in Subchapter S corporations can now be made without transferring voting rights.

Prior to the new act, all shares of stock in Subchapter S corporations had to have the same voting privileges. If the company president wanted to give stock to his children, he had to grant them the same voting rights he enjoyed. But the Subchapter S Revision Tax Act changes this, permitting the corporation to issue shares with various levels of voting power. Now the company president can issue non-voting stock to his children, allowing them to share in the ownership but not in the management.

• Tax-free income earned by a Subchapter S corporation on its investments can, under the new law, be passed through to shareholders free of federal taxes.

"Before, if the corporation invested in tax-free instruments, the interest from the investments was tax-free to the corporation," says an Ernst & Whinney tax manager. "But once that interest flowed to the shareholders, it became taxable as dividends. Many shareholders weren't aware of this and therefore found themselves with more taxable income than they thought they had. Now that income will stay free of federal tax."

• When the Subchapter S corporation has a bad year, its losses may be carried over to offset gains in future years.

For federal taxes, Subchapter S losses have been deductible on the personal returns of the shareholders, but only to the extent of their loans and investments to the firm. Assume a sole shareholder's investments and loans to the corporation totaled $20,000 but the firm lost $30,000. Under the old law, that $10,000 could not be recouped. With the new act, the loss can be carried over indefinitely. Should the shareholder invest or lend an additional $10,000 or more, he can use the carryover loss to offset future gains.

Still, there are drawbacks to the Subchapter S form. The corporation may have to pay state taxes, and some state laws may conflict with Subchapter S benefits. A firm incorporated in various states may want to take a different course in each.

The best approach is to review the issues with an accountant or tax attorney. See if the new law makes Subchapter S status right for you.

20

Government Offers More Than $1 Billion in Innovation Grants

THE great technology hunt is on. Uncle Sam is in the market for a better mouse trap and is giving small business a chance to deliver the goods.

It's all part of the Small Business Innovation Development Act, legislation designed to encourage small-company participation in national research and development projects. The act requires federal agencies with external R&D budgets of $100 million or more to set aside for small business a gradually increasing share of the funds, rising from a low of .1 percent in 1983 to 1.25 percent in 1987.

"It is hoped that the money will stimulate small business's innovative capacities," says the Small Business Administration Administrator for Innovation Research and Technology. "This could produce important benefits for small companies and for the country. Studies have shown that small business is far more innovative per employee than is large business. Small firms have been responsible for important innovations including xerography, insulin, and the gyrocompass."

Federal agencies will dispense grants through programs modeled after the National Science Foundation's long-established Small Business Innovation Research program. Note the following guidelines:

• Companies interested in obtaining innovation grants contact the SBA for a list of participating agencies, including the kinds of research they will be funding. Write the SBA, SBIR Program, 1441 L Street, NW, Washington, DC 20416.

• Applicants identify the agencies most likely to support their R&D projects, filing with each a program solicitation form outlining the type of technology the company is working with, how it will be produced, and its commercial applications.

• Proposals accepted for phase I grants receive up to $50,000 for conceptual work, including preliminary designs and feasibility studies. A company developing an energy-saving device would use the funds to conduct chemical analyses or to prepare technical drawings.

• The most promising concepts are selected for phase II grants, which provide up to $500,000 for product development. Here, the technology starts to take shape. The energy-saving device, for example, moves from drawing board to prototype.

• In phase III, a campaign is launched to attract private capital to the project. Government funding ends but the sponsoring agency may contract to purchase quantities of the newly developed high-technology product. The technology may also be sold on the commercial market.

• Companies may apply for an unlimited number of grants and they may mix private capital with government funding at any stage of the development process. The federal grants are limited to companies with a maximum of 500 employees.

21

How Bankers Evaluate Small Business

THEY are rich, powerful, influential, competitive, and secretive. They are the nation's banks, and for all their visibility little is known about their most important function: approving and rejecting loans. To prospective borrowers, who gets how much and why remains a mystery.

But small-business owners can peer behind the pin-stripe curtain, discovering how bank officers evaluate loan applications; why one firm secures a $100,000 line of credit while another equally profitable venture comes up empty-handed; and why one loan has to be backed with collateral while another goes unsecured.

"Prospective borrowers should know how a bank evaluates a small business," says the vice-president for small business accounts at a major money center bank. "This can help them to be more successful in the initial loan application and in the quest for additional funds. Although banks do not have a single set of hard-and-fast rules for passing on loan requests, we do rely on the so-called five Ps—people, purpose, payment, protection, and perspective. Strength in all of these key indicators is likely to produce a favorable decision."

Loan officers review the five Ps for the following signs:

• Management personnel experienced in their field or industry and with good credentials for running a profitable venture. The emphasis is on a solid track record, both as a professional manager and a reliable credit risk.

Because the small-business owner typically wears so many hats, he is more crucial to the company's success than his counterpart in the Fortune 500. That's why bankers feel so strongly about documenting management's capabilities. It is best to present a detailed résumé, credit history, and objective third-party endorsements from sources familiar to the bank. Applicants without previous business experience may draw on personal references.

"One of the biggest mistakes small companies make is to waltz into a bank, unknown and unannounced, and ask for a loan," says the executive vice-president of a lending institution specializing in small-business accounts. "It is always preferable to have a prominent source—be it an attorney, accountant, or another business person—pave the way for the initial visit. This formal introduction gives the prospective borrower an advantage because he comes as a known quantity and with the recommendation of an established contact."

• What the money be used for. The bank must believe that the loan will be put to a valid business purpose—one with good prospects for success.

"Even an experienced manager can go off on a tangent," the bank V.P. says. "No matter how successful a borrower has been in the past, we won't fund his newest venture to market ice cubes in Alaska. The bank must have confidence both in the owner and the enterprise."

Here, too, solid documentation may sway the bank's decision. A market research study or a consumer poll can convince the lending officer that there is demand for the applicant's product or service. Investing a few thousand dollars in this documentation may prove pivotal in landing a million-dollar loan.

• Although no one has a crystal ball, borrowers are expected to demonstrate that they will be able to repay the loan from operating profits. Financial reports, including profit and loss statements for the past three years and cash-flow projections for the term of the loan, can be helpful.

"These reports should be prepared by a CPA firm respected by the bank," a banker advises. "In a way, the small company is judged by the company it keeps. If the financials are prepared by CPAs that have a reputation for shoddy work, our respect for the applicant and our confidence in its reports are very low. Should a company want the names of reputable CPA firms, most bankers will be pleased to provide them."

22

How Banks Decide On Small-Business Loans

I N the mating game between small business and the banks, business pursues while bankers choose. For every company that lands a loan, dozens are turned down. Successful suitors are those the banks believe are in the best position to repay on time and in full.

Just how this is determined goes to the heart of the business-bank relationship and has broad impact on which small companies survive and which fail for lack of capital. Although bankers are eager to make loans and want to work with applicants to win approvals, more companies have their hands outstretched than there is money to go around. The question is, how do successful applicants stand out from the competition? What do banks look for in approving and rejecting loans?

"Often it boils down to the company's ability to provide adequate collateral," says Dale W. Lutz, vice-president of Manufacturers Hanover Trust. "Although we

evaluate the firm's personnel, the purpose of the loan, and
the company's ability to repay, can be a swing factor. It is
incumbent on management to determine what kinds of
collateral it can offer and to make this known to the bank.
Acceptable forms of collateral include property, securities,
inventory, and receivables."

An executive vice-president of Sterling National Bank
adds that those loan applicants seeking funds for a start-up
venture can pledge initial orders as a form of collateral.

"Many of our borrowers are former salesmen or
engineers who left their employers to start companies of
their own. Although these fledgling entrepreneurs tend to
be high-risk borrowers, we may work with them, providing
they demonstrate the ability to service bank debt. For
example, if the prospective borrower lands a major order
for his product or service, we may be willing to lend him
the money to service that order."

The last of the conceptual criteria banks apply to loan
applications is perspective. This means that all of the factors
relating to the loan must make good business sense when
viewed together.

"A new restaurateur who previously worked for a
major hamburger franchise may have difficulty getting a
loan even if he has good management skills and a sound
credit rating," Lutz explains. "When he opens his own
restaurant, it may be situated between a McDonald's and a
Burger King. Judging the applicant by the standard criteria,
they may come up fine individually but not when viewed
from the standpoint of perspective. We want to make
loans—that's our business—but there has to be good
likelihood of repayment."

Banks also base borrowing decisions on quantitative
measures pertaining to the applicant's profitability and
liquidity. Decisions are made, in part, on the basis of
lending ratios.

"One of the measures of profitability—net income as a percent of sales—is considered a key indicator of the borrower's financial performance," says vice-president of the Mercantile Trust Co. "Acceptable percentages range from 1 percent for low-risk, low-capital-requirement businesses to 15 percent or more for high-risk, capital-intensive ventures."

Liquidity, an analysis of the company's ability to generate sufficient cash to pay its bills, is often measured by the current ratio, figured by dividing current assets by current liabilities. Bankers look favorably on ratios of 1.5 to 1 or better.

"But a poor ratio doesn't automatically exclude the borrower," the Mercantile Trust V.P. advises. "The ratios are only starting points for asking additional questions. If we find that the ratio can be improved by restructuring short-term debt into long-term obligations or by attracting additional equity capital, it may be possible to make the loan. A key point is that small firms with unacceptable ratios may be able to work with their banker or accountant to make improvements in their financial standing and thus qualify for the needed funds."

23

Negotiate Loans: Here's How to Get the Best Terms

IN the David and Goliath dealings between small business and the banks, borrowers believe they have to take what the bankers dish out or take nothing at all. But that's not true. Even the smallest firms can negotiate for loans, winning concessions on many of the key terms.

While the inexperienced focus only on the amount of money at stake, savvy borrowers pay close attention to the fine print. They know that the rules of the agreement can have a major impact on the cost of the loan and its effectiveness in helping the firm grow.

"Negotiating for the most favorable terms can make the difference between a successful loan and one that produces less than management had hoped for," says a partner with Touche Ross, CPAs. "Borrowers should never accept a standard agreement form from the bank without making major changes. The trick is to know which terms should be negotiated and what to ask for on each."

Consider the following guidelines for negotiating bank loans:

• Try to avoid pledging the company's stock as collateral. This will give the lender effective control of the firm should it default. A wiser approach is to pledge assets such as equipment or real estate.

• If the negative covenants restrict management's ability to raise additional long-term debt or prevent the sale or merger of the business, try to win the right to pay off the loan without penalty. This gives management more leeway to take advantage of breaking opportunities. Should an attractive merger partner present itself, for example, the company will not first have to pay points on the outstanding loan balance.

• Provisions should be made to lift restrictions on paying dividends, acquiring company stock, or boosting owner and employee salaries if the company exceeds a stated amount of after-tax profits.

"Let's say the firm registers a 50 percent increase in profits from one year to the next," the Touche Ross partner explains. "Well, that's exceptionally good performance by anyone's standards. The company should be allowed to pay salary increases or to declare dividends to the owners."

• Substantial limitations on the incurrence of additional debt should be revised according to future increases in the company's net worth. Here again, the borrower is rewarded for its good performance.

• Fight hard against absolute restrictions on additional debt. Try to win a cushion of at least 25 percent more than what you think your capital needs are. Quite often, capital projections fall well below actual requirements.

• Never assign casualty insurance proceeds to a lender. The money will be needed for repairs and for operational capital during the downtime. This concession may, however, be difficult to get on equipment and building financings. One approach is to agree to maintain the assets and to repair or replace them with the insurance proceeds.

• If there is a limit on capital expenditures, get the annual amount to be cumulative. For example, if the annual limit on the purchase of fixed assets is $100,000 and the company only spends $50,000, it should be permitted to spend $150,000 the following year.

• Provisions prohibiting the sale of a "substantial" part of assets should be spelled out to state precisely what "substantial" means. Seek approval to sell up to 10 percent of the assets.

• Negotiate for annual, semi-annual, or quarterly payments. Extending beyond the standard monthly payment schedule gives the borrower longer use of its money and improves cash flow.

Accountants and business attorneys can help to negotiate loan agreements.

24

How to Boost Your Borrowing Power

S MALL companies thirsting for growth capital can boost their borrowing power by using subordinated debt. This creative money-raising technique combines some of the key features of both debt financing and equity financing.

Typically, bank loan agreements set limits on the amount of additional debt borrowers may acquire from other sources. This restrictive covenant can limit a small company's growth potential. Just when more capital is needed to fuel expansion, the bank exercises its veto on additional loans.

"But they'll often permit subordinated debt," says Herbert C. Speiser, a partner with the small-business practice of Touche Ross & Co., CPAs. "That's because it is considered junior debt and it takes a back seat to the bank's claims. In most cases, subordinated debt cannot be repaid until the bank's senior debt is retired. The key to getting the banks to agree to additional borrowing is to show that their interests will not be jeopardized in any way."

An executive vice-president of Sterling National Bank agrees. "Additional borrowing is automatically acceptable to us providing it is subordinated to our loans. Once we have reached a lending limit and another source wants to provide subordinated financing, that's just fine. The problem is that many business owners want to put the new debt on equal standing with ours. That we won't accept."

Private investors, venture capital firms, and Small Business Investment Corporations (SBICs) are often willing to provide subordinated debt because it is coupled with so-called equity kickers, usually in the form of warrants. These instruments enable lenders to acquire shares of stock in the companies they finance. That's the trade-off of subordinated debt: the acceptance of greater risk in exchange for the opportunity to achieve a greater return in the form of capital appreciation. If the small company performs well, the provider of subordinated debt shares in its success.

"Our members are willing to extend subordinated debt to those firms that exhibit strong growth potential," says Walter Stultz, president of the National Association of Small Business Investment Companies.

"The SBICs need some indication that the equity kicker will have real value. That's how they profit from the investment. Growth firms are usually seen as a good bet."

The use of subordinated debt can provide numerous benefits:

• Because many lenders view subordinated debt as part of the firm's equity base, the addition of this long-term financing can make the company eligible for more bank borrowing. The debt-to-equity ratio—one of the key measurements banks use in setting loan amounts—is substantially improved.

• Subordinated debt agreements often call for interest-only payments in the early years of the loan. Principal payments may be delayed for up to five years or more. Interest rates and pay.ent schedules are negotiable and can be tailored to the company's needs.

• By obtaining concurrent medium-term bank loans and subordinated debt, the company can pay down its short-term borrowing and can add significantly to working capital.

"But there are drawbacks," Speiser adds. "The borrower may be giving up a piece of his business to outside investors and he may be locking up funds that cannot be removed until the senior debt is repaid."

Companies interested in securing subordinated debt should make certain that the terms of the agreement are acceptable to the senior lender. Have an experienced business attorney and an accountant structure the transaction.

25

Creative Financing Can Help You Buy Business Property

IN today's economy, home buyers and business owners face a common problem: how to leap the hurdle of high interest rates. For both, creative financing may be the answer.

Put simply, this means finding an alternative to the traditional bank mortgage. With creative financing, property sales are structured so the terms are affordable to the buyer and acceptable to the seller. The strategy is applicable to virtually every type of real estate, from the split-level home to the retail store.

"Although the term 'creative financing' has been bandied about by residential brokers, the concept really has greater potential when applied to business properties," says Leonard Primack, a financial consultant specializing in real estate deals. "By using any number of government programs and financing techniques, property transactions can be executed at well below prevailing interest rates. This is especially important for small businesses because so many cannot afford to carry mortgages of 16 percent or more."

Consider the following creative strategies for purchasing commercial real estate:

• Determine if the property's existing mortgage is assumable. If so, this can reduce interest costs on a portion of the purchase price.

• Try to convince the mortgage holder to increase the assumable portion by renegotiating the underlying interest rate through a "blending."

"Let's say an individual wants to buy a business property that has an assumable 8.25 percent mortgage for 25 percent of the purchase price," Primack explains. "The bank may be willing to increase that assumable portion to 50 percent providing the rate for the entire amount is stepped up to say 12 percent, with the right of renegotiation every five years. This way the lender gets out from under its old 8.25 percent mortgage and the buyer gets a new mortgage that is still far below market rates."

• Apply for a Small Business Administration 503 loan. This secondary mortgage is available for up to 40 percent of the property's financing to a limit of $500,000.

The SBA sells debentures in the money markets to finance its 503 mortgages. Interest rates to property buyers are slightly higher than the bond coupon and are fixed for the term of the mortgage. This gives buyers an opportunity to lock in at least part of their interest costs. SBA 503 mortgages range from fifteen to twenty-five years.

"Because this mortgage program is relatively new, a lot of companies don't know that it is available to them," says an SBA executive. "But most businesses small enough to qualify for SBA loans are eligible for 503 financing. They should apply at SBA-certified development companies, which actually dispense the mortgages. SBA district offices can help applicants find the development companies that are authorized to work with them."

• Companies with good credit ratings can obtain up to 100 percent financing by selling "industrial revenue bonds." Under this procedure, local development authorities can authorize companies to sell tax-free bonds to raise money for property purchases.

Typically, the bonds are sold to banks or insurance companies, have maturities of from ten to twenty-five years, and carry floating interest rates that are well below the prime.

"We turned to industrial revenue bonds to finance the purchase of a previously leased facility," says the president of a small cookie-making company. "The procedure worked extremely well. We raised $770,000, which was 100 percent financing, at an interest rate that floats at 25 percent below prime."

Accountants, bankers, and commercial real estate brokers can help structure creative financing strategies.

26
How to Refinance Loans

C APITAL is the fuel that keeps companies growing. To keep pace with demand, emerging ventures need a steady diet of cash for materials, plant, and equipment. No sooner does management land a loan than the call goes out for another.

There are several ways to deal with these growing pains. Companies that have an outstanding loan or mortgage, but still find themselves short of capital, can refinance the existing loan or obtain a new loan and leave the existing loan unchanged. Just which approach the business takes can have a dramatic impact on repayment schedules, cash flow, and interest rates.

"Although lenders must be willing to go along with refinancing schemes, small businesses should recognize that they have some leverage in getting what they want," says a CPA with Deloitte Haskins & Sells, the national accounting firm. "If the company has an old, low-interest loan, it may be able to convince the bank to refinance it with a larger, higher-rate loan. This certainly helps in the effort to get more capital. But the borrower must determine that the new rate is not too high to negate the benefit of giving up the existing low-interest loan."

The best approach is to study the relative merits of new loans and refinancings to determine which is best for your business and to work with lenders in designing a suitable financing package. Consider the following:

• Companies carrying two separate loans may be faced with higher current loan payments than those borrowers choosing to refinance outstanding balances.

Assume Company A has a ten-year equipment loan for $50,000 and needs another $50,000 to purchase a new machine. In today's market, banks are unlikely to extend the new loan for more than five years, unless it is part of a refinancing. If the note is issued for a short term, the annual payments will be higher than if the two loans were combined and paid out over ten years.

"Another key point is that the borrower's willingness to refinance the old loan at a higher rate may be the only way he'll qualify for another long-term fixed-rate loan," the CPA adds. "Although banks have generally stopped offering this type of financing, they may be willing to do so just to rid themselves of the old loan and to trade up to a higher rate. That's what we mean by using your leverage to get the most favorable terms."

A vice-president of the Bank of America agrees that banks are willing to negotiate on virtually every aspect of business financing. "This is the age of imaginative lending," the banker notes. "Banks are trying to improve the yield on their assets, so they are open to various financing options. Although most are wary of fixed-rate commercial loans, they will reduce the spread above prime on floating-rate loans if a low-interest note is extinguished in the transaction."

• Borrowers refinancing outstanding loans must look both at the new loan's "stated" and "implied" interest rates. The company may actually be paying more than the quoted rate indicates. That's because in a refinancing, the rate on the outstanding loan is changed.

For example, assume Company B is making annual loan payments of $10,000 plus interest at 10 percent. When the balance is $30,000, the lender agrees to replace the existing loan and advance an additional $30,000 in exchange for a $60,000 note payable over six years with a 15 percent annual interest rate. But because the old 10 percent loan is retired, the implied interest rate on the incremental $30,000 is more than 17 percent, rather than the quoted 15 percent. The implied rate is the true cost of refinancing.

• Another option best suited for companies that do not need additional financing is to prepay an outstanding low-interest loan in return for a reduction of the principal.

"Take the hypothetical case of a company with an existing $100,000 fifteen-year loan at 8 percent interest," the CPA explains. "If the principal balance now stands at $64,000, the bank may be willing to retire the note at approximately $52,000. The company saves $12,000 and the bank puts the principal to more profitable use. It more than makes up for the discount by making higher-interest loans to other borrowers."

Small-business owners may profit by discussing with their bankers the wide range of refinancing options.

27

Hybrid Financing Offers Loans and Equity

SMALL companies shopping the market for business financing may find an unfamiliar product on the shelves. A growing number of cash sources now offer hybrid plans that combine the key features of loans and equity capital. The mix may be ideal for fledgling ventures blessed with good growth prospects.

A single financing transaction may have two different components. The loan portion allows for temporary use of funds in exchange for interest payments and a commitment to repay the principal according to an established timetable. Experts view this simply as renting money. The equity position, on the other hand, is a capital investment made in return for shares of stock. By taking this "equity kicker," the financial institution has the opportunity to earn substantial profits if the company prospers. This carrot may prompt lenders to flash the green light for loans they might otherwise reject.

"Recently, a company in the greeting card business asked for our help in acquiring one of its competitors through a leveraged buyout," says a vice-president for C.I.T. Commercial Finance Co. "Although they were pledging the acquired firm's assets to secure the loan, there wasn't enough collateral to cover the purchase price. But when the owners offered us 5 percent of the company's stock, we agreed to do the deal. We even reduced the interest rate on the loan portion by a half percent.

"We are getting into these combination financings because our competitors are starting to offer them and because this kind of transaction enables us to work with companies that might not qualify for standard borrowing. To date we've been limiting this activity to acquisitions, but we would entertain equity deals for any number of business projects."

Small Business Investment Companies, a national network of privately owned financial institutions licensed by the Small Business Administration, are extremely active in hybrid financing. Most seek to develop a portfolio of investments in small, dynamic companies.

Although loan/equity terms are open to negotiation, SBICs commonly use three types of financing to fund small business:

• Loans with warrants. In return for a loan, the small business issues warrants enabling the SBIC to purchase common stock in the company, usually at a favorable price, during a specified period of time.

• Convertible debentures. The SBIC lends the small business money and in return receives a debenture. The SBIC can either accept repayment of the loan or convert the debenture into an equivalent amount of common stock.

- Common or preferred stock. The SBIC purchases common or preferred stock from the portfolio company.

The Walter E. Heller Co. brings together two of its divisions to structure loan/equity deals, resulting in yet another source of hybrid financing. "Our loan department may ask our venture capital division to take the equity position in a financing of this type," says a Heller vice-president. "Although we do not actively promote this kind of transaction, we do it from time to time. And it can help companies unable to qualify for standard loans to get needed capital."

Still, experts warn against viewing equity kickers as loan provisions.

"Small-business people must recognize that when they accept equity investments, they are giving up part of their company," says Herbert C. Speiser, a partner with Touche Ross and Co., CPAs. "They have to recognize that they will be sharing ownership with outsiders. Some lenders disguise this by calling it 'extra interest.' In these deals, lenders take a percentage of a company's sales over a certain base figure. No matter what they call it, that makes them a partner.

"I generally advise against equity financing unless the company cannot raise money any other way. If that's the case, it's wiser to share ownership of the business than to have no business at all."

28

How to Make a Loan to Yourself

T HE best loans are those a company makes to itself. By using sophisticated cash management to postpone accounts payable and speed up collections, any business can squeeze extra value from its money. The net effect is like getting an interest-free loan.

The idea is to strike a delicate balance between the obligation to pay vendors and the incentive to keep cash in the company's accounts. This is the essence of savvy cash management: it makes maximum use of company funds without jeopardizing the firm's credit rating.

"If you can accelerate the receipt of funds, you can reduce the need to borrow to meet the company's cash requirements," says an audit manager with Touche Ross & Co., CPAs. "And if you can keep those funds in your account for extended periods, you can use the money to pay down existing debt. In either case the benefits of sound cash management can be equivalent to that of an interest-free loan."

Among the dozens of cash management techniques available to small business, some are widely known, others are rarely utilized. Experts suggest that business owners explore these dollar-stretching strategies:

• Ask your bank for an account analysis as well as a monthly statement. The analysis views the account the way the bank sees it. Is it profitable? Are there substantial cash balances for the bank to invest?

"Two key components of the analysis—the sum of collected and uncollected balances—are revealing," the CPA adds. "If collected funds—those that have been cleared through the Federal Reserve—far exceed the amount required to cover the bank's minimum balances and fees, then the bank may be profiting at the customer's expense. The sophisticated small business will make an arrangement with the bank for the excess funds to be shifted into a sweep account where it earns high interest in the money market. Chances are that unless this arrangement is made, the bank will invest the money for its own account and keep the interest."

Although some banks may be reluctant to provide account analyses, others will respond to a bottom line appeal. Tell the bank that you want to maximize cash management opportunities and that you will sever other banking relationships in return for the major bank's cooperation in achieving this objective.

"One of my clients boasted that his bank named his company as their eighth most profitable account," says one CPA and small-business specialist. "My response was that he was doing something wrong. Some of that profit should have been his."

• Establish a company lock box at the local post office. Have customers send payments to the box rather than the company's business address. A bank assigned to service the box gathers all the mail, separates the checks from the paperwork and immediately deposits the money in interest-bearing accounts. The box may be serviced up to several times a day as well as on weekends.

"The fee for this service, which usually varies with the number of transactions involved, is more than made up for by the amount of extra income the company earns by putting its money to work as quickly as possible," the CPA adds. "Quite often, when the small firm makes the deposits itself, the checks sit around in the mailroom or in various offices waiting for the paperwork to be completed. This means money down the drain. Any small firm with a substantial volume of checks coming in—including busy professional practices—can profit from a lock box arrangement."

III

CREATING WEALTH— YOUR PERSONAL FINANCES

29

New Look at Tax Shelters

S UCCESS in business brings the universal complaint that Uncle Sam claims half the rewards. To defend against this silent partner, the self-employed invest billions in real estate, oil drilling and equipment-leasing tax shelters. All work on the same theory: it's not how much you make that counts but how much you keep.

But are tax shelters good investments? Do investors keep more income by investing in shelters? Have recent tax law revisions changed the rules of the game? Which shelters have survived congressional reform and when is the best time to invest in them?

Accountants and attorneys specializing in tax shelters have one of those "good news, bad news" answers. On the bright side, they report that shelters are still alive and well and effective in helping the self-employed cut their tab to the federal treasury. But in the same breath they warn that the range of acceptable shelters has been drastically

reduced and some of the most attractive investments of
recent years are now discredited.

"This is an excellent time for those interested in tax
shelters to update themselves on recent developments,"
says a director of tax policy for Arthur Andersen, CPAs.
"The government has taken a harder line on exotic shelters
designed primarily for tax avoidance. These deals generally
have little or no economic substance: nothing short of a
miracle will earn the investors a profit.

"The law discourages investments in exotic shelters by
requiring that all tax positions be based on 'substantial
authority' and that the taxpayer have a 'reasonable belief
that his tax treatment is more likely than not the proper
treatment.' Failing this, the taxpayer may be liable for a
penalty as well as back taxes plus interest should the shelter
be disallowed by the Internal Revenue Service. The
problem is, the government action raises more questions
than it answers. What is 'substantial authority' or 'reasonable
belief'? No one really knows. This makes it hard to tell
when and where the penalty will be applied."

Another problem with tax shelters is in the minds of the
investors. Most people misunderstand a basic element of
shelter economics. That is, they can lose money even if the
write-off is two or more times the amount of the
investment. The common misconception is that if a $10,000
investment yields a $20,000 deduction, the tax benefit alone
covers all the risk, and there is nothing to lose even if the
shelter does not produce a dime of income.

"But that's not true," says one CPA/attorney. "Tax
shelter deductions are only deferrals that must be taken as
income sometime in the future. If a tax shelter is invested in
an apartment house and the project turns out to be a total
loss, the investor may have to take back as income the
amount of the write-off in excess of his investment. In a bad
deal, this can be like a time bomb waiting to explode."

Current tax shelter restrictions apply not only to the terms of the investment but also to the impact it can have on total earnings. Successful business owners and professionals will find that another legal provision, the alternative minimum tax, can require payment of a tax even if the individual has sufficient deductions to cover 100 percent of income.

"The alternative minimum tax puts a limit on so-called tax preference items such as intangible drilling costs in oil and gas tax shelters," the Arthur Andersen CPA explains. "Regardless of what the shelter promoters say, individual taxpayers may not be able to take advantage of all the investment's tax benefits. Just how much can be claimed depends on the taxpayer's total income, deductions, and credits."

Bleak as this picture may appear, there are opportunities beyond the caveats. Experts believe that by drawing lines around the most abusive shelters, the government has established a limited safety zone for time-tested plans—mostly in real estate, oil and gas, and leasing—with modest write-offs and sound economics. Providing these tests are met, shelters can still offer current tax benefits and capital gains.

In the search for the ultimate tax shelter, two key factors come into play: good timing and a wide-angle view of the options. Those who shop the market and invest before the year-end rush get the best mix of write-offs and capital gains.

"There's a general rule that the longer you wait to invest in a shelter, the less chance you have of finding a really good one," says Mitchel Feinglas of the Asset Management Group, investment advisers. "The problem is that the most active investors in tax shelters, the self-employed, are so wrapped up in running their businesses that they postpone personal financial planning until the closing days of the year. But by that time the best shelters are sold out.

"When is the best time to invest? Spring through early fall. Taxpayers wise enough to act in this period get to choose from the cream of the shelter crop. What's more, by investing early they can generally claim a greater deduction than if they wait until December."

Currently, the emphasis is clearly on proven shelter concepts, mostly in oil and gas, real estate, and equipment leasing. Attorneys and accountants specializing in tax shelters offer the following guidelines:

• Oil and gas. With the energy business in a slump, shelter activity has switched from speculative exploration and drilling programs to more conservative oil completion funds which focus on incremental production from proven wells.

"The write-offs are more modest—often less than one to one," one investment advisor notes, "but much of the income is tax free. I look at the completion funds as a sort of municipal bond with more upside potential."

Adds a tax partner with Arthur Andersen & Co., CPAs, "Tax shelters tend to move in and out of fashion, often reflecting developments in the tax law and the economy in general. Until recently, the syndication of drilling rigs was the rage. Shelter promoters promised substantial tax benefits to those who invested in this very expensive equipment used to pump oil from offshore fields. But with the decline in the oil markets, many of these rigs are sitting idle, producing neither oil nor income, and the promoters are off selling more fashionable deals. The caveat is not to be so dazzled by the tax benefits that you ignore the economics."

• Real estate. Most popular because it is the exception to the "at risk" rule, real estate is the only category of shelter that allows investors to deduct an amount greater than their personal liability in a deal. With other shelters, a recourse note must be signed for the amount of the write-off that exceeds the actual investment. Because real estate does not require this, it provides for greater leverage. A $10,000 investment can produce a write-off of $20,000 or more, in some cases with good economics.

"From my viewpoint, the best real estate deals today are in shopping centers and garden apartments," Feinglas advises. "That's because you want the opportunity to sell for capital gains somewhere down the line, and modest properties are more marketable than huge office towers. Certainly, there are more qualified buyers for a suburban mall than for the World Trade Center. This limits the risks and may provide for a faster return of capital."

• Equipment leasing. With equipment leasing deals, limited partnerships purchase everything from word processors to rail cars and lease them out to third parties, using the tax benefits to shelter income.

Although the concept is sound, investors are advised to do their homework on the kind of equipment being leased. High technology devices, such as computers, are subject to rapid obsolescence. This may cause a sharp decline in current values and resale potential.

"In every category of shelter there are good deals and bad deals," the Andersen partner warns. "While no single criterion can be used to distinguish one from the other, one universal rule does apply. If the shelter seems too good to be true, it probably is."

30

How to Boost the Yield on Business Ownership

T HOUGH it is often said that owning a profitable small business is like having a key to the mint, many successful entrepreneurs find themselves cash poor. With all of their worldly wealth tied up in corporate assets, they are unable to support a standard of living that reflects their achievements. But there are ways of increasing the owner's current return without draining the firm of needed capital.

The best strategies for accomplishing this seek to maximize tax deductions and to make savvy use of fringe benefits. The laws provide entrepreneurs with attractive perks not ordinarily available to wage earners. Cashing in on these opportunities can provide business owners with thousands of dollars for living expenses, luxuries, college tuition, or personal savings.

"A substantial number of our clients—owners of closely held corporations—complain that they just don't make enough money," says a partner with Main Hurdman, CPAs.

"When we hear that complaint, we focus first on the amount of money they are taking as salary and as dividends. In most cases, we advise that they take more of the former and less of the latter. That's because salary is only taxed once, at the personal level, and dividends are taxed twice, at the corporate and personal levels. What's more, salaries are tax deductible to the corporation while dividends are not.

"By getting a deduction at the corporate level, you need to earn less money to pass through every dollar to the shareholders. You need twice as much in earnings to go the dividend route as to go the salary route. Although the Internal Revenue Service demands that the owner's salary be reasonable, inflation has prompted the government to be more liberal in judging what is reasonable compensation. Small-business people should review their salary levels in light of this."

Experts suggest the following additional strategies for getting more out of a business:

• Establish a medical expenses reimbursement plan. The Tax Equity and Fiscal Responsibility Act has tightened the rules governing personal medical expense deductions, allowing only that amount that exceeds 5 percent of adjusted gross income.

But with a corporate medical expense reimbursement plan, the business owner submits medical bills to the corporation and is reimbursed in full. The corporation, in turn, takes a tax deduction. Such plans must be offered to employees on a non-discriminatory basis.

• Donate shares of a company's stock to a charity and have the corporation repurchase the shares at their market value. The charity gets a cash payment for the stock and the individual gains a tax deduction. Assuming the shares are worth $10,000, the 50 percent taxpayer has a $5,000 savings as well as the satisfaction of supporting a worthy cause. One caveat is that there should not be a binding obligation for the corporation to buy back the shares.

• Establish a Subchapter S corporation. With this structure, all income flows directly to the shareholders, completely eliminating the problems of dividends and corporate taxes. Again, the single taxation rule allows for more after-tax income.

• Seek reimbursement for the use of an employment-connected home office.

"Should the business owner use part of his home to conduct company affairs, he may be reimbursed by the company for expenses associated with this space," says a tax partner with the accounting firm of Seidman & Seidman. "This payment is essentially tax free because there are expenses to offset the income. But several tests must be met to qualify for this deduction. Most important, the home office must be used regularly and exclusively for business, including visits by customers and other business contacts."

• Have the corporation purchase automobiles, convention travel, and entertainment when this can be shown to have a legitimate business purpose. Anything the company pays for that would otherwise come out of the owner's pocket clearly boosts his total return.

Work with an accountant in structuring business and personal financial strategies.

31

Foreign Investors Are Buying U.S. Small Businesses

SMALL-BUSINESS owners seeking to sell or merge their companies may find ready buyers overseas. Attracted by America's social and political stability, foreign investors are committing millions of dollars to the acquisition of U.S. firms.

"European buyers have always been active here but the trend is now accelerating and is attracting capital from all parts of the world," says an executive with The Geneva Corp., consultants specializing in business sales. "Chalk this up to economic turmoil outside of the U.S. When investors worry about conditions in their own countries, they look for safe havens and many still consider America as the place the last capitalist will do business. While these people once focused on big businesses, they are now buying even the smallest outfits from a half million dollars and up."*

* Contact Geneva Corp. at 2923 Pullman, Santa Ana, CA 92705. Tel: (800) 854-4643.

Foreign capital, which flows most heavily from the United Kingdom, favors acquisitions in real estate, high technology, proprietary products, and other small firms positioned for rapid expansion. Investors excited by the dynamics of U.S. markets typically prefer to buy small businesses as platforms for growth rather than building entirely new companies from scratch.

"One overlooked benefit of selling to foreigners is that they are often in position to pay more for the business than an American of equal means," the executive says. "That's because unlike the U.S., many nations treat goodwill as a deductible item.

"Take the business with assets of $500,000 that is selling for $1.5 million. A foreign corporation acquiring that company may depreciate the goodwill, thereby using the tax benefit to subsidize the cost of the acquisition."

Brokers specializing in small-business sales claim that owners bringing their companies to market domestically or overseas fail to present their firms in the best possible light.

"Typically, the owner of a privately held company wants to suppress earnings in order to minimize taxes," the executive explains. "But when he goes to sell that firm, he forgets that the prospective buyer wants to see the highest possible earnings. It's important to remember that the seller is selling a business but the buyer is buying an investment.

"To make that investment look as attractive as possible from an investment standpoint, we suggest recasting the company's financial reports by restoring all of the owner's bonuses and perks—including company cars, boats, and club memberships—and replacing them with a straight salary figure that would be paid to a non-owner in a similar capacity. We want to show prospective buyers what the firm is capable of earning were it not drained by the entrepreneur."

Companies are also advised to update the value of their fixed assets. Buildings and equipment carried on the books at original cost may have appreciated over the years, making them worth many times the stated sum. Corporate acquirers are always attracted to these "hidden values."

Another expert specializing in foreign sales, Neil Wassner of Main Hurdman, CPAs, notes that European companies buying American businesses are interested in both consumer products and industrial markets.

"In many cases, they are seeking to acquire U.S. firms that distribute their products here. This gives them the opportunity to control their channels of distribution. We recently concluded a sale of an American pipe importer to an Irish company that makes the pipes."

Companies interested in exploring the market for foreign buyers may seek a free listing in Main Hurdman's publication, "Companies Available for Sale," which is distributed, through the firm's partners, to prospective buyers around the world. Write Neil Wassner, Main Hurdman, Park Avenue Plaza, New York, NY 10055.

32

How to Pick Small-Business Stocks

T HERE'S more than one way to make money in small business. Most do it by rolling up their sleeves and running a company; others prefer to let their brokers do the work. They buy and sell small-business stock.

Different as these approaches are, there is a common thread. Knowing what makes small businesses succeed can reward investors and entrepreneurs alike. A prominent money manager specializing in small-company stocks claims that those with an experienced eye can profit handsomely by buying and selling these often overlooked securities.

"The best investment in America today is in small business," says Charles Allmon, publisher of the newsletter *Growth Stock Outlook* and a money manager whose stock portfolios are invested in small company issues. "While most people hardly keep up with inflation by investing in what I call the 'blue gyps,' those who know how to identify successful small companies see their money grow rapidly. Some of the top fifty companies in the U.S. were selling for more in 1960 than they go for today. If that's not a gyp, I don't know what is."

In contrast, a small company Allmon recommended in 1965, Texas Oil & Gas, has soared from 50 cents to about $40, adjusted for splits and dividends.

"That kind of performance is pretty much limited to small business," Allmon adds. "There are risks to this approach but they are greatly reduced if you know how to analyze small companies and gauge their potential."

Allmon's small-business stock selection strategy is based on the following rules:

• Avoid high technology stocks. Although the standard advice for small-business investments is to favor the high tech issues, Allmon considers them to be a dead-end street.

"They are not really growth companies. They light up the sky like Roman candles only to burn out in a few years, leaving the investors with losses. My preference is for companies with long-established markets."

• Avoid the small-company stocks everyone else is throwing their money at. Spot these situations by their high price/earnings ratios. Never buy anything with a price/earnings ratio of over 25 and only go that high for exceptional opportunities. In most cases, stay within the 8 to 13 range.

• Look for companies that can expand in good times and in bad. When considering an investment, determine if the firm can grow without interruption for the next five or ten years. The key criterion: Do its products or services seem to have long-term appeal or are they just another fad?

    • Examine the firm's financial position. Buy signs include little or no long-term debt, a substantial amount of cash or other liquid assets, a 20 percent to 30 percent return on shareholders' equity, and a current ratio of assets to liabilities of two to one or better.

    • Invest in companies that service the high-tech sector but are not themselves high-tech based.

    "While I stay away from the small computer manufacturers," Allmon explains, "I favor companies that provide the computer industry with more or less staple products. These firms are not so vulnerable to rapid obsolescence. One company, for example, makes disposable computer forms. It has plenty of growth potential but it won't be damaged by the shakeout that will soon eliminate some of the computer makers. It will continue to serve the survivors."

    Certainly, Allmon's system is not foolproof. Years ago he decided against recommending H&R Block when it was still an emerging venture, believing it could not achieve sustained growth. Still, the gainers appear to outnumber the losers.

    "When we decided to diversify part of our portfolio, we gave Allmon $5 million to invest for us," says one client. "In the three years since he's been serving as a money manager for us, the assets have increased in value by 70 percent. In the beginning, some of the trustees were uncertain that small-business stocks could really pay off. There are few doubters left."

33

How to Preserve Capital

THERE'S more to financial success than just making money. The greater challenge, many say, is preserving capital through the years. Unless entrepreneurs consider both components of financial success—creating and maintaining wealth—they may find that the profits earned from business ventures are here today, gone tomorrow.

In a volatile economy, money in the bank may be a sitting duck for runaway inflation; assets in a brokerage account may be ravaged by a skidding stock market. Capital tied up in corporate retirement plans, Keoghs, and IRAs is especially vulnerable to these threats. To protect their long-term investments, the self-employed must cushion them against economic cycles.

The traditional approach is to diversify holdings in a broad range of financial instruments. This, the theory holds, makes for a balanced portfolio: bad news for stocks may be good news for bonds; the risk of a major setback is dramatically reduced.

But a growing number of investment advisers now contend that simple diversification does not go far enough. To successfully protect retirement and other long-term portfolios, diversification must be structured according to fixed percentages.

"Investing for long-term gains and capital preservation takes discipline," says the president of an investment advisory firm. "The investor must refrain from jumping on the bandwagon every time there's a brief run-up in the price of stocks, bonds, or precious metals. The best way to build this discipline into the individual's investment program is to allot a set percentage of funds for each of several investment options and stick with those percentages over the years."

Adds a noted investment adviser, "A sensible investment strategy accepts that the future is unknowable and then sets out to profit from that future. One strategy for hedging against all foreseeable risks is to diversify into a broad cross section of investments and to assign to each a fixed percentage of the funds available for investing. This effectively protects the investor from risking and perhaps losing a substantial portion of his retirement portfolio on speculative flings."

Experts offer the following guidelines for making long-term investments based on the percentage-diversification strategy:

• One bull on the stock market's long-range prospects recommends a two-part diversification: 50 percent of the funds in long-term government bonds and 50 percent in stocks.

"I like bonds for income and security, and the stock market for dividends, to be reinvested, and for capital appreci ion. Assuming there's $100,000 to invest in stocks, I would spread this over twenty different issues. All should be more exciting than the blue chips but less dicey than penny stocks. Those with little feel for the market may want to invest in a growth stock mutual fund."

• A consultant to the Permanent Portfolio, a novel type of mutual fund designed specifically for capital preservation, suggests that the fund's percentages may offer the ideal protection against economic crises.

"The Permanent Portfolio divides its capital into six investment categories: gold (20 percent), silver (5 percent), Swiss franc assets (10 percent), real estate and natural resource stocks (15 percent), common stocks and warrants (15 percent), and U.S. government-backed instruments (35 percent). I believe this balance—which investors can duplicate on their own or by buying shares in the fund— provides extraordinary protection while still allowing for profit potential."

A vice-president of retirement plans for Merrill Lynch cautions that investment percentages and the selection of specific investments must be tailored to the individual's age, income, and other personal considerations.

"In general, I recommend 20 percent to 50 percent in equities and the balance—no more than 20 percent for each—in any combination of long-term corporate bonds, intermediate-term bonds, unit trusts, certificates of deposit, and money market funds."

Investors are advised to work with experienced accountants and financial planners in reviewing the pi Js and cons of fixed-percentage investing and in structuring portfolios on this basis.

34

Company Savings Plans Build Nest Eggs

THE move to make Americans spend less and save more may be aided by a little-known plan that allows for the tax-free accumulation of thrift dollars. Small-business owners and their employees can salt away substantial nest eggs.

It is all made possible by so-called qualified employee savings plans. Savings contributed to these plans grow quickly because the interest is untouched by Uncle Sam until withdrawal. The plans are designed to encourage employees to save part of their earnings for retirement. Thrift is rewarded by the employer's matching contributions and by the tax incentives.

"Corporate savings plans are typically part of profit-sharing plans," says a tax manager with the national accounting firm of Deloitte Haskins & Sells, "but they are not as well known as the latter. The major difference between them is that the employee must contribute to savings plans in order to participate. The advantage to this is that all participants have an active stake in the program and the costs are shared between the company and the workers. Small businesses should certainly explore these fringe benefit options."

The fruits of the savings plan are passed along to the small-business owner's personal finances. As an employee of the corporation, he too can make qualified deposits matched by company contributions. The interest on the owner's savings is also shielded from taxes. What's more, the company's contributions to the plan are tax deductible.

"Savings plans can be a good mechanism for amassing cash," the tax manager adds. "Assume the owner of ABC Corp. is forty years old and earns $50,000 a year. If a plan is set up with a 6 percent employee contribution and a 3 percent employer contribution, a total of $4,500 or 9 percent of his salary may be invested.

"At age 65 retirement, the owner's account will show total contributions of $112,500, investment income (based on 10 percent compounded annual rate of return) of $330,062, a total savings of $442,562."

Savings plans share the typical eligibility requirements for qualified profit-sharing plans. In order to get the tax benefits, the plans cannot discriminate in favor of highly paid employees. Although seasonal and part-time staffers, those with less than one year of service, and those below age 21 may not have to be included, other employees must be eligible to participate in the plan.

To ensure that the plans do not discriminate against low-level employees in rule or in practice, the Internal Revenue Service generally limits its approval to those plans calling for employee contributions of 6 percent or less. This limitation is based on the assumption that low-salaried workers cannot afford to save a greater percentage of their earnings. It must be pointed out, however, that the uniform rate of contribution does enable the owner and other highly paid executives to put away more money in absolute terms.

Employer contributions to the savings plans may match employee contributions by any ratio determined by management. Companies may, for example, match worker contributions dollar for dollar, double them, or cover them by 50 percent. The only restriction is that the employer's contributions are tax deductible to a maximum of 15 percent of all eligible employees' compensation.

Vesting schedules may also be determined by the company. Full and immediate vesting gives participants non-forfeitable rights to the employer's contributions. Plan design can make these benefits payable at or before normal retirement age.

Attorneys may be hired to set up corporate savings plans and to write the trust agreements. Or owners may participate in prototype plans available through banks and insurance companies. Either way, CPAs should review the tax aspects and should be consulted on the fundamental question of whether a savings plan is a good fringe benefit for the company.

35

How to Choose an Executor

C AN a family business survive the founder's death? Can it pass smoothly to the heirs or be sold to the highest bidder? If a skilled executor is in charge, the answer is probably yes.

Put simply, executors administer the disposition of estates. All too often, small-business owners assign this key role to the first friend or relative willing to take it on. But that's a mistake. What does Uncle George know about running a business? Can he keep it alive long enough for new management to take control? Probably not. His incompetence jeopardizes the estate's biggest asset.

Professional executors—mostly banks and trust companies—specialize in preserving and distributing assets as the deceased intended. They bring legal, business, and financial skills to the task. Most important, they are certain to be around while Uncle Harry may not.

"Uncle Harry may be ill, dead, or otherwise engaged just when the family business needs his attention most—

immediately after the owner's death," says a senior vice-president of the United States Trust Co. "The firm is most vulnerable then and could suffer without the proper stewardship. That is why it is essential to appoint an executor who will be here today, here tomorrow."

It is never too early to hire an executor. Experts advise that every business owner should have a will and a professional assigned to carry it out. Consider the following guidelines in selecting and working with a competent executor:

• Make certain the professionals are well versed in tax matters. Distributing assets through trusts and other tax-wise instruments can save substantial sums of money.

"Many people think that it is best to leave all of their assets to the surviving spouse, but that may not be true," says an executive with U.S. Trust's estate planning department. "Assume an estate of $1.2 million and the husband and wife die after 1987 when the amount sheltered from federal tax is equal to $600,000 for each individual.

"If the first spouse to die left all to the survivor, there would be no federal tax on that estate. However, in the second estate, $600,000 would be taxable, as only one half would be sheltered from tax. Assuming the second spouse did not remarry, the federal estate tax on this amount would be $235,000. But if the first spouse had instead left only one half to the survivor and the other half in trust for the survivor's benefit, the amount in trust would escape taxation in both estates. The $235,000 would be saved."

• If an attorney or accountant is deeply involved in the operation of the business, consider appointing that person as a fiduciary along with a bank or trust company.

This may provide continuity in planning for the company's future.

• When more than one party is named as executor, make certain that the mix of individuals and institutions can work effectively as a team. Most important, they must be able to make fast and effective decisions.

• "Consider naming as executor the trust department of your company's commercial bank," says a partner with Price Waterhouse, CPAs. "This way the bankers most familiar with the company's business affairs will be readily available to the bankers administering the estate. This can be more rewarding than choosing a trust company simply because it has a prestigious name."

• Be prepared to pay an executor's fee of from 2 percent to 5 percent of the value of the estate. Larger estates of more than $1 million are at the lower end of the fee spectrum.

• Recognize that the rules governing estates—including the work of executors—are governed by state law. In most cases, business owners with interests in various states are subject to the laws of the state in which they make their primary residence.

IV
SLASHING EXPENSES

36

Audits Win Refunds, Slash Business Costs

THE newest kind of audit on the business scene today has little to do with the arcane science of CPAs. This one's bottom line–oriented and likely to present you with a hefty refund check in a matter of weeks. It ferrets out overpayments to the likes of Ma Bell, wraps them up in a ribbon, and returns the money to your account. Launch an audit and chances are you'll be looking at a lump sum return of $25,000, $50,000, or more. Found money, any way you look at it.

The auditors base their services on a simple notion: with the increasing complexity of telephone charges and electricity rates many businesses cannot keep track of what they are paying for. Confused by detailed printouts—by strange jargon and numeric codes—they act on faith, writing a check for the full invoice amount. But blind faith it is: the vast majority wind up enriching the vendors to the tune of 5 percent to 40 percent in excess payments. Like tourists in a foreign land, they simply hold out their money for the cabbie to collect the fare—and take all he wants.

But all is not lost. The new breed of auditors scours payment records for as far back as five years, checking for overpayments and winning refunds for the full amount. By specializing in a given industry, audit firms can read between the lines, finding errors a layman wouldn't know to look for. Most auditors are former insiders of the utility and insurance firms; they use their firsthand knowledge of the system to make it work for you.

Typically, auditors work on a contingent fee basis, commanding 50 percent of the refunds secured for their clients. All you do is sign a form granting the auditors access to your records and then sit back and wait for a check. There may be a small fortune coming your way.

Refund auditors are active in the following fields:

Electric Utility. Auditors analyze clients' energy-consumption patterns, usage trends, billing charges, and complete service costs and then compare this data with the local utility's rates and classifications. The objective is to win retroactive refunds and to reduce client bills by eliminating errors, duplication, and improper rate designation.

Among the auditors' key strategies:

- Taking advantage of off-peak discount rates.
- Switching the firm from one commercial category to another that offers a lower rate.
- Eliminating charges for closed or discontinued operations.
- Analyzing all charges on a monthly basis and identifying computer or policy errors.

"Most companies don't realize that there may be alternative billing plans and classifications available to them," says a senior executive with Consumers Utilities Service. "They start out in business with a certain rate basis and never think of having that changed even though changes in their operations may qualify them for significant savings. Management must keep in mind that utilities are not obligated to put their customers in the lowest rate category—that's the user's responsibility."

Adds the manager of a laundry and dry cleaning firm, "Electric utility auditors have returned thousands of dollars to us. That's money that would have gone down the drain without their help."

Telephone. Charges are commonly made for telephone equipment that does not exist. Every line, switchboard, and telephone has a separate charge. The billing for this can be confusing. Auditors break down the equipment charges, check that all equipment is on the premises, and make sure that the rates are accurate.

"A full 60 percent of the companies we audit pay more than they are supposed to for telephone use simply because they don't know when they are being overcharged," says Robert De Rosa, president of Bridging the Gap Through Communications, an auditing firm.

Telephone company bills rarely provide detailed information on local calls. It is therefore difficult for management to check on charges for this service. As a result, errors made in billing local calls tend to remain on the phone company books for years.

"The wrong message unit rate is often levied against local calls," De Rosa adds. "We rectify this by requesting a computer printout of the call activity, breaking down all the calls by individual number and making certain that all charges are appropriate. Mistakes here can really add up. We saved one office $51,000 on this."

Errors in the billing for Yellow Pages advertising can also result in substantial overpayments. Rate schedules are complex and are subject to constant change. Auditors make certain that bills for the advertising reflect the actual size of the ads and the current rate.

Says an executive with a small bus company, "When I called in the people from Bridging the Gap Through Communications to review our telephone billing, they found among other things that we were being billed for a connection that had been removed 18 years ago. They won for us an immediate refund of $6,000 and helped to lower our regular monthly statements by about $80."

Names of reputable auditors may be obtained from accountants, consultants, and trade associations. Those quoted here service clients nationally and may be contacted at Consumers Utilities Service, Bergenfield, NJ 07621, 201-387-7400; Bridging the Gap Through Communications, Blauvelt, NY 10913, 914-359-7600.

Here's a personal angle: the benefits of refund audits can extend to your home telephone and utility bills. Wise business managers will use their leverage as audit clients to win an audit of personal finances. Simply ask the auditor to review your residential electric bill while they're doing the company's. Telephone consultants found that one small-business owner had been charged for five years for an extension phone he never had. Thanks to the auditor's findings, he no longer makes donations to Ma Bell. What's more, he won a tidy personal refund of $168—enough for theater tickets and dinner for two on the town.

The money is yours. Go out and get it.

37

How to Cut Property Taxes

S MALL companies hunting for ways to save money should set their sights on property taxes. Experts claim that one of every four commercial property owners is overtaxed and eligible for substantial reductions. Thousands of dollars are at stake.

Tax appeal specialists represent small companies in the fight to retrieve excess tax payments and to net long-term savings based on reduced assessments. The appeal firms, which range from local real estate appraisers to large outfits serving clients across the nation, review property assessments and advise if a claim is in order.

"Many commercial property owners think they are being fairly taxed but are actually paying more than they have to," says the president of Management Associates, Inc., a property tax consulting firm. "That's because they look at only one of the factors that go into an assessment, judge it to be accurate, and conclude that the tax is right. But the fact is that several components generally contribute to an assessment and if just one is overlooked the reason for seeking a lower tax may not be evident.

"For example, take a newly constructed office building that is only partially rented. Because there is no historical income stream, the assessor may base the tax solely on the property's cost of construction. This may be unfairly high. To win a tax reduction, we review the income and expenses of comparable properties and develop a 'stabilized income approach.' If we can prove that this should serve as a major basis for the market value, we may win a tax reduction."

Appeals begin with a comprehensive property review. Owners provide information on the property's cost, date of purchase or construction, income flow, building plans, and the most current tax bill. The consultants analyze this in the context of local tax policies. Should this indicate that the owner is being overassessed, the appeal begins at the most immediate taxing authority and moves, if necessary, through the court system.

Firms specializing in property tax appeals generally handle everything from the initial review to the litigation. Some accept contingent fees, claiming 50 percent of the tax saving. Others demand a flat fee based on the amount of time spent on the case. The major objection to set fees of course is that they must be paid even if the case is lost.

"But many owners are still better off with the flat fee," says one real estate appraiser. "There are two benefits. First, if there's a big refund, the appraiser is not an equal partner in the owner's settlement. His share is limited to the amount specified up front. Also, contingent fee outfits are tempted to exaggerate claims in order to net themselves bigger fees. That can get the case thrown out."

One consultant, whose firm works on contingent and flat fee bases depending on the size of the claim and the client's preference, disagrees.

"The method of payment has no bearing on how an appeal is conducted. We are successful in 90 percent of the cases we accept, be they for set fees or commissions. On average, the client's tax bill is reduced by 25 percent. In dollar amounts, these reductions have ranged from $2,000 to $400,000."

Successful property tax appeals can bring dual benefits. Property owners win cash refunds on excess taxes paid from the date the appeal is launched and the revised assessment reduces future taxes.

"We have learned from experience that tax authorities often overassess properties," says a vice-president of a real estate development firm. "Tax appeal specialists know how to spot the errors and get the tax bills reduced. They have saved us thousands of dollars."

Contact real estate brokers and accountants for the names of reputable tax appeal specialists. Make certain that firms operating nationally are familiar with state and local tax policies.

38

Co-op Subsidies Stretch Advertising Budgets

SOMETIMES entrepreneurs wish for miracles like finding ways to double the power of advertising budgets. Well, that's a wish that can come true.

Co-op advertising makes it happen. This budget-stretching technique helps small companies increase advertising exposure without increasing costs. Management simply applies for cash subsidies available from thousands of product makers and distributors. These marketers—mostly large corporations—generally match advertising expenditures on a 50/50 basis. For every dollar the small business spends in support of the marketer's brands, the co-op sponsor pays 50 cents, up to a specified ceiling. The subsidy is designed to boost local promotions.

"It has never been more important for small companies to make effective use of advertising," says a vice-president of a co-op processing and research firm. "Co-op offers a pool of $6 billion annually to do just that. The problem is, co-op programs are often burdened with complex rules.

Companies confused by the finer points may wind up with less than their maximum allowance."

But this can be corrected. A computer analysis of thousands of co-op claims reveals that a few common problems account for the lion's share of unused funds. The following tactics can help companies detour the pitfalls on their way to claiming a windfall of co-op dollars:

• Demand that manufacturers provide a written description of their co-op programs and refuse to sign sales agreements until this is revealed. Some manufacturers do not promote the availability of co-op funds, or mention it only to select accounts. But refusing to make a deal without this information always brings it to the surface.

• Submit media bills before the forty-five- to sixty-day deadline established by most co-op programs. Advise media representatives that your invoice must be received before the specified date. Claims submitted after the deadline may be rejected.

• Do not accumulate advertisements for the purpose of making one large claim. The faster claims are submitted, the faster they are paid.

• Integrate co-op funds throughout the company's ad campaigns. Avoid force-feeding the money into a brief spurt of media spending.

"Many retailers forget about their co-op funds until the last month of a co-op program," the VP adds. "They quickly run as many ads as possible so they won't forfeit their co-op dollars. But this haphazard approach is often ineffective. Co-op accruals should be spent wisely—at the right time, on the most salable products, in the best media. With this in mind, it is good to borrow your vendor's advertising theme and schedule. He spends enormous sums of money to find the ideal ways to reach the ultimate consumer."

• Don't settle for the standard 50/50 co-op split without inquiring about the manufacturer's most favorable terms. Some co-op vendors offer reimbursements totaling 100 percent of advertising costs, enabling the small company to advertise for free. The most generous deals are usually limited to seasonal promotions and new product introductions.

"One of my vendors pays 100 percent of my advertising costs up to a specified maximum," says the president of a swimming pool company. "I qualify for this by ordering products in advance of the big sales season and by giving large orders. It's well worth the effort. I wouldn't be able to advertise as heavily without co-op money."

Never avoid complicated co-op programs just because they are hard to follow. Ask the manufacturer or a media sales representative for assistance in putting the co-op program to work for you. It's a rare opportunity to get something for nothing.

39

How to Buy Business Telephones

W HERE once there was order, now there is confusion. Where there was monopoly, there is competition. Where there was a single price—take it or leave it—there are price wars. It's the world of telecommunications and it's changing faster than the speed of sound.

Once a tranquil protectorate of the giant American Telephone and Telegraph Company, the telecommunications market is now a hotbed of competitive activity. Dozens of aggressive marketers selling everything from long distance lines to computerized equipment are out to put a telephone on your desk, a microprocessor in your switchboard. This billion-dollar battle benefits telephone users, including small businesses, but it also raises a number of difficult questions.

Ever since the Federal Communications Commission opened the floodgates by allowing private industry to compete with Ma Bell in the sale of telephone equipment, businesses have faced three major decisions: whether to leave Bell for a competitor, which competitor to choose, and whether to buy equipment or lease it. Today, with AT&T focusing more of its attention on equipment marketing through its newly launched American Bell subsidiary (nicknamed Baby Bell), the questions and choices are more perplexing than ever.

"No doubt, this is a most confusing time in the telecommunications market," says Robert DeRosa, president of Bridging the Gap Through Communications, a telephone consulting firm. "Bell is saying one thing and doing another. Competing companies are making claims and counterclaims. Small business, which is caught in the middle, doesn't know what to make of it all.

"There is, however, a silver lining here. All the news about changes in the telecommunications market has prompted companies that lease from Bell to rethink their policies. They are trying to determine if they can save money by purchasing equipment and if they'll have to accept any negative trade-offs in the process."

But let's start at the beginning. How does a company shop for telephone equipment? How does management gauge its communications needs? What does it look for both internally and in the equipment marketplace?

"It is best to go about the process much as a business would shop for a computer," says a director of Information Systems Consulting Services for the national accounting firm of Main Hurdman. "That's because today's phone systems are similar to computers in many ways. They have hardware and software components, they are subject to obsolescence as new technology is developed and they require significant capital investments."

Consider these guidelines for selecting and purchasing telephone equipment:

• Conduct a survey of the company's communications needs, projecting the number of employees that will be required to have telephone instruments over the next five years. Select an expandable system capable of accepting increased capacity as the company grows.

• Give equal consideration to the vendor's service capabilities and his equipment specifications. Because the telephone system is the company's link to the outside world, disruptions in service can lead to bottlenecks, lost orders, and snares in customer relations. To avoid this, obtain independent verification from consultants or business associates that the vendor is financially sound, is authorized by the manufacturer to do service work, and has a good track record in maintenance and repairs.

• Shop the market, asking three to five vendors, including American Bell, to propose an efficient communications system. Select the system that best matches your company's needs.

Do not base the final decision on price alone: look for the ideal mix of fair price, superior equipment, and top quality service.

• Base the buy/lease decision on the economics of a given deal rather than a universal rule that one approach is better than the other.

"Although purchasing offers the dual benefits of depreciation and investment tax credits, vendors providing their own lease packages may do so at such attractive terms that leasing turns out to be most economical," the Main Hurdman partner explains. "Telecommunications vendors, much like automobile manufacturers, are competing on financing rates as well as equipment prices. Companies in the market to acquire equipment may want to take advantage of this."

• Review all existing Bell system arrangements with an eye toward finding a more cost-efficient alternative. Most experts agree that long-time Bell customers now leasing equipment should invite vendors, including American Bell, to submit bids for alternative systems and financing terms.

DeRosa claims that "In the vast majority of cases, the move away from Bell and toward the purchase of a competitor's system will save the company a substantial sum of money. For example, when a New York law firm asked us to suggest an alternative to their Com-Key 718, we recommended an Omega III system produced by a Japanese firm. The lawyers had been paying Bell $725 per month for a system that had only fourteen instruments and no microprocessor. But with the Omega equipment, they now have 24 lines and a computerized element, and the cost is only $408 per month for sixty months. After this payment period, they will own the equipment outright."

But the switch to Bell's competitors may pose problems.

"We had to suffer through a difficult time immediately after changing from Bell to another system," says the publisher of a suburban newspaper. "There were lots of bugs in the system. Calls were disconnected and we had a hard time getting a dial tone. Happily, the system works well today. Although there are some hidden charges for servicing—which we didn't have to pay with Bell—we are saving a lot of money overall. For us, owning our telephones has proven to be a cost-efficient change from the old leasing arrangement."

Small companies hopelessly confused by the options in buying and leasing telecommunications equipment may want to work with a consultant. These experts guide business clients in the selection, installation, and use of telephone systems.

That's the good news; the bad news is that choosing a consultant also takes a bit of homework. Some consultants are truly independent; others are tied to manufacturers through questionable sales agreements. The best approach is to work with a consultant whose total allegiance is to the telephone user. This breed rarely sells equipment but simply acts as an adviser in the selection process and oversees the installation.

Consultants can be paid by the hour or on a project basis. To design, select, and supervise the installation of a twenty-five-instrument system, count on a fee of between $2,500 and $5,000.

Contact accountants and trade associations for the names of reputable consultants.

40

Employee Ideas Can Cut Business Costs

T HE old saying "You have to spend money to make money" may be equally true when it comes to savings. By paying cash awards for employee suggestions, management may tap a rich lode of better ideas that can cut the company's costs and bolster its bottom line.

The thinking goes like this: Those at the front lines are best positioned to spot a company's flaws and to recommend more efficient methods of operation. Enlightened management must find a way to tap this source of information—to make employees partners in the drive for greater productivity and higher profit margins.

"One proven approach is to establish a mechanism for communicating employee ideas to top management, for evaluating those ideas and for paying awards to the responsible employees," says a spokesman for the National Association of Suggestion Systems, a Chicago-based trade association." The cost of administering this system and paying the awards is modest when viewed in the context of the savings it is likely to produce.

"For example, a survey of 190 of our member companies found that every dollar they invested in suggestion plan systems returned five dollars to their businesses. This represented an aggregrate savings of about $700 million."

Although suggestion systems are often associated with major corporations, they are equally effective and generally easier to install in small businesses. The National Association of Suggestion Systems offers the following guidelines:

• Announce the plan to the employees, explaining in writing how it works and how they can benefit from it.

• Designate an executive to administer the plan and to evaluate suggestions. The job demands a strong-willed individual familiar with the company's immediate and long-term objectives.

• Ideas can be submitted through office correspondence or a simple suggestion box.

• For each idea accepted by the company, pay the responsible employee a flat fee, generally ranging from $500 to $5,000, or a percentage of the first year's savings.

"With the percentage approach—which varies widely from company to company but averages 17 percent among our members—it is a good idea to set a maximum award," says NASS executive secretary Oliver S. Hallett. "Failing this, the company may have to pay enormous awards for the 'golden nuggets' that yield very substantial savings. A million-dollar idea could produce an award liability of $170,000. That's probably far more than the company wants to pay. Setting a fair ceiling on percentage awards will not diminish employee incentive."

- Respond to each suggestion, informing the employee of the company's decision and the reason for it.
- Establish an appeals procedure enabling employees whose ideas are turned down to present their suggestions to a more senior executive or to the company owner.
- Keep complete and accurate records of all transactions relating to the suggestion system. This will help to insure the proper allocation of awards and to prevent the duplication of payments.
- Be aware that the suggestion system may constitute a contract with the company's employees. Management must be prepared to pay the sums specified in the award schedule.
- Have the company's attorney review the suggestion system before it is introduced to employees.
- Determine, in advance, the objectives management hopes to achieve. Suggestion systems can generate high levels of enthusiasm and productivity as well as tangible cash savings.

"Our system has accomplished what it was set up to do twenty years ago," says the suggestions administrator for Magnetic Peripherals, Inc. "It has brought valuable employee recommendations to management's attention. Our best idea—a suggestion for changing from one type of cable to another in the production process—has saved us $239,000. For that, we paid our maximum award of $1,000."

41

BOPs Make Good Buy in Business Insurance

BUSINESS ownership carries two kinds of risk: the insurable and the kind only prayers can answer. Because the former is eminently more reliable, prudent entrepreneurs seek to cover their risks with a fistful of commercial policies. The idea is to pay more and pray less.

But are they getting their money's worth? Experts say it depends on how the coverage is structured. Insurance may be purchased in monoline policies, which provide separate coverage for each category of protection, or in multiperil form, which offers a wide range of coverage in a single policy.

"One type of multiperil protection—the Business Owner's Policy—provides comprehensive coverage for the small firm's risk exposure at a fraction of the cost of an equivalent group of monoline policies," says the president of an insurance brokerage firm. "Because BOP policies have become widely available only in recent years, many small firms still haven't purchased this kind of package coverage. But in virtually every case, they'd be getting more insurance at a lower price."

BOP offers economical protection by spreading the carrier's risks to a wider pool of policyholders. With monoline policies, every buyer of vandalism coverage, for example, is likely to be in a high-risk community and thus subject to repeated cases of vandalism-related damage. But with BOP policies—most of which include vandalism protection as a standard feature—the coverage is extended to a universe of high- and low-risk policyholders. The projected loss ratio is reduced, as are the premiums.

BOPs are generally available in basic and broad form plans. Typical policies, which vary by carrier, include the following features:

• Basic BOP insures buildings and contents against named risks such as fire, lightning, wind, hail, and vandalism; provides general liability including legal responsibility for a fire, property damage, and advertising liability; and contains business interruption coverage, which compensates for the loss of business income resulting from an insured peril.
• Broad form extends property coverage to all risks minus standard exceptions including wars and floods; full crime coverage is added, including losses due to theft, employee dishonesty, counterfeit currency, and extortion; dollar limits on liability and business interruption are increased.

Broad form is widely viewed as the best buy. A relatively small increase in premiums brings a substantial boost in coverage. At one carrier, the cost differential between basic and broad form for a retail shop in a major metropolitan city is $275 a year, a 20 percent increase for superior protection.

Specialized policies—designed for specific businesses and industry groups—can give BOPs a customized feature. Carriers active in the small-business market have introduced BOPs for pizzerias, Chinese restaurants, real estate offices, pharmacies, and others.

"Every type of business has its own unique risks and concerns," says a supervising underwriter for Travelers Insurance. "Specialized BOPs, like the one we designed for pizzerias, respond to this. Because these shops do a substantial volume of take-out business, they are vulnerable to telephone breakdowns. So we've added telephone interruption coverage to their BOPs. Should telephone service be interrupted, we reimburse them for the income loss resulting from this."

But BOPs may not blanket a company's risk exposure.

"They may provide inadequate coverage for goods in transit, boiler and machinery, company-developed software, and peak season inventory," the underwriter warns. "To fill in major gaps, management should compare a checklist of its risks to all features of BOP coverage and should then adjust the BOP or purchase additional lines of insurance."

Independent agents can help the self-employed select the best mix of insurance policies.

42

Postal Service Reps Can Help Cut Your Mailing Costs

A SK small-business owners to name their pet peeves, and complaints about the mails usually head the list. Gripes range from high costs to slow service to bureaucratic indifference. But help may be a phone call away.

That's all it takes to summon one of the more than 600 customer service representatives located throughout the postal system. Specially trained to help businesses make effective and economical use of the mails, these experts recommend money-saving procedures that can slash thousands of dollars from annual postal costs.

"The more we know about companies' needs and the more they know about our services, the more both sides benefit," says an assistant postmaster general for customer service. "That's the theory behind the customer representative program. We try to interface our facilities with commercial mailers' needs and capabilities.

"It's surprising how many well-managed firms are unaware of the diversity of postal services. That's why many conduct their mailings inefficiently. Our goal is to correct this through information and instruction. Using the services of our customer representatives is like having consultants at your disposal free of charge."

It works like this. A company seeking postal assistance starts by calling its local postmaster. Simple requests for information may be handled on the spot; for more elaborate problems, customer representatives are dispatched to the company's place of business. The representatives review the firm's mailing procedures with an eye toward recommending more efficient alternatives.

The following are popular strategies:

• Have manila envelopes printed with green borders. Business mailers often complain that first-class letters sent in large envelopes take a week or more to reach their destination. This happens when mail handlers mistake the large pieces for third-class advertising mail, which moves at a lower priority. The green border, recognized as a symbol for first-class mail, helps to ensure proper handling.

• Use Presort to cut first-class postage from 20 cents to 17 cents per letter. To qualify, companies prepare mailings of at least 500 letters by Presort specifications. The letters must be grouped by zip code and posted by meter, precanceled stamp, or permit imprint.

"A sound approach is to have the company's computers generate billing labels in zip code order," says a Postal Service general manager. "That way the major Presort requirement is performed automatically."

• Reserve the use of Express Mail, an overnight service, for those letters and parcels that must arrive the next business day. Less urgent packages can travel at the lower-rate priority mail, which is generally delivered within three days.

"There's no doubt that the customer service representatives know their business and know how to make you a more effective mailer," says a credit manager for the Book-of-the-Month Club. "They've helped us correct mistakes and they've put us into the Presort program, which is definitely saving money."

Certainly, there are limitations to the customer service program. Some of the most nagging postal problems are caused by bureaucratic inefficiencies that cannot be rectified by a change in mailing techniques. What's more, some of the best mailing services are offered by private couriers, an option Postal Service representatives are not likely to recommend. It is a good idea to call on these firms for a complete view of your company's mailing options.

V

FUELING PROFITS

43

Cash Parking Lots: Short-Term Investments That Pay Big

TODAY, even money has to work for a living. Corporate cash held on account for business expenses, tax payments, or dividends must be invested for short-term gains, turning what was once an idle asset into a profit center. This strategy generates incremental income that goes straight to the bottom line.

The results can be extraordinary. Assume ABC Co. collects $250,000 on a major sale. Knowing that an equivalent sum will be due on a mortgage balloon payment within six months, management may deposit the income in a standard checking account until the payment date. But by investing the $250,000 in a short-term instrument, the firm can earn more than $10,000 on the value of its cash.

"Any business that still retains big balances in checking accounts is selling itself short," says Mitchel Feinglas, a registered investment adviser with Asset Management Group. "Money is worth too much today to let it collect dust. When the prime rate was 6 percent, the drive to make short-term investments was not that great because the rewards were only marginal. But with the onset of a double-digit prime, business was compelled to make productive use of every dollar. Well-managed companies should have no idle cash."

A smorgasbord of short-term investment vehicles— known as cash parking lots—offer small companies a wide range of risk/reward options for turning money into more money.

"Generally speaking, the higher the risk associated with an investment vehicle the higher its yield," says Robert Morello, vice-president and manager of taxable securities sales for Manufacturers Hanover Trust Co. "Management must determine how much of the former it is willing to accept in order to gain more of the latter. One viable approach is to invest in a number of instruments providing a mix of risks and yields."

Consider the following options:

• 85 Percent Dividend Received Funds are mutual funds designed exclusively for corporate rather than individual investors. These little-known vehicles offer the opportunity for high yields, capital appreciation, and excellent tax benefits.

The funds invest in a portfolio of common and preferred stocks. Because most corporations can deduct on their federal income tax returns 85 percent of the dividends they receive from other domestic corporations, earnings from the funds are taxed at a low effective rate.

"Corporate shareholders in our Qualified Dividend Fund pay a maximum of 6.9 percent on their dividends," says an executive with the Fidelity Group, mutual fund managers. "This is calculated by subtracting 85 percent of the return—thanks to the corporate dividend exclusion—

and applying the top corporate tax rate of 46 percent to the balance.

"For example, corporations investing $100,000 in our Qualified Dividend Fund, at a 10 percent yield, would earn gross income of $10,000. Of that, $8,500 would come off the top, leaving a net taxable income of $1,500. At the 46 percent tax rate, that would produce a tax of $690 or 6.9 percent of gross income."

The same corporations investing $100,000 in a fund without the 85 percent dividend exclusion feature would pay taxes of $4,600 on a $10,000 gross return. To equal a Qualified Dividend Fund's yield of* 10.14 percent a corporation in the highest tax bracket would have to find a fully taxable investment yielding 17.48 percent.

One caveat is that corporate mutual funds are vulnerable to losses. Should the value of a fund's portfolio decline, so too will its net asset value (and per share price). Although fund managers try to limit this risk by investing in stable companies with solid earnings performance—electric utilities are among the favorites—negative results are possible. On the plus side, however, a strong stock market may boost the fund's net asset value, rewarding the investors with profits.

Because these funds are subject to cyclical swings and are therefore less predictable than other investment options, small-business owners may want to limit use of them to cash reserves that can be invested for six months or more. Investments may be arranged through brokers or mutual fund sales representatives.

• Money market funds, the most popular alternative to standard checking accounts, invest in any number of corporate obligations, government instruments, and certificates of deposit.

*For comparison purposes only. Yield is subject to change.

The key attractions are convenience and liquidity. By writing checks on current balances, companies can benefit from the "float." Cash in the fund continues to earn interest until the check clears.

Widely regarded as safe and stable investments, money market funds do, however, carry some risk. The greatest drawback in the minds of many investors is that they are not insured. To compensate for this, fund managers have developed a hybrid that invests exclusively in U.S. government-guaranteed securities. The trade-off here (remember the ever-present risk/reward formula) comes in the form of lower yield.

• The onset of bank deregulation has made certificates of deposit for $100,000 or less more flexible instruments for short-term corporate investments. Because the new rules allow for negotiated rates and terms, CDs can be custom-designed to meet a company's cash requirements. Should the depositor want to invest $90,000 for 86 days—to coincide with an income tax payment date or a real estate closing—many banks will write CDs for that specific period. One approach is to shop three to five banks, selecting the one with the highest yield coupled with FDIC insurance (which provides protection up to $100,000).

Harvey Moscowitz, a partner with Seidman & Seidman, CPAs, suggests a clever way to maximize CD yields. "Withdraw the interest monthly and reinvest it in a money market fund. This way the company earns interest on its interest. Most depositors make the mistake of leaving the interest in the certificate."

• Commercial paper—a form of unsecured promissory notes—is issued by bank holding companies and industrial corporations. Yields and risks generally exceed those of CDs.

Commercial paper is backed only by the issuer's underlying credit. Quality paper is rated A1,P1 (the most secure) and A2,P2. Investors can check Moody's or Standard & Poor's ratings before making a purchase. Maturities range from one day to 270 days with minimum investments generally starting at $50,000.

"Because commercial paper is generally sold on a discounted basis, companies using it for cash parking lots can back into the amounts they'll need at maturity," Morello explains. "For example, if a company needs $100,000 in 45 days to meet tax obligations, it can buy 9 percent 45-day paper for $98,875. With interest, this will pay $100,000 at maturity."

Commercial paper is available through the issuer, banks, or securities dealers.

• Treasury bills—short-term instruments backed by the full faith and credit of the U.S. government—are sold in minimum $10,000 units with $5,000 increments. Ranging in terms from one day to one year, T-bills offer lower yields than CDs but are more liquid. They may be sold before maturity to banks and securities dealers.

"A fundamental rule of short-term investing is to look at the difference in yields between T-bills and commercial paper," Feinglas notes. "If the difference is less than one half percent, all but the largest investors are probably better off with T-bills. That's because the underlying risk in commercial paper—the possible failure of the issuer to honor its commitment—is not a real problem with T-bills. The federal government has one thing General Motors doesn't: access to the printing press. If Uncle Sam gets in a bind he can print more money to honor his debt."

• Eurodollar time deposits, one of the least known short-term investments, offer one of the highest risk/reward profiles.

"These are non-negotiable U.S. dollar deposits domiciled in a bank or bank branch outside of the U.S.," Morello explains. "Maturities range from overnight to six months with minimum investments starting at $100,000. Eurodollar time deposits are illiquid investments—in most cases funds may not be obtained before the maturity date—but yields usually exceed those of commercial paper."

Some investment advisers are uncomfortable with Eurodollars.

"In these uncertain times, I advise against Eurodollar investments," one advisor warns. "T-bills, through lower-yielding, make for a sounder investment because they are backed by Uncle Sam. It is important to remember that cash parking lots should earn money for the business investor without subjecting the firm to undue risk."

Two additional factors may modify the underlying objective of investing maximum sums for maximum yield:

• Active borrowers may want to keep certain amounts of cash in checking accounts to satisfy bankers' demands for compensating balances and to build goodwill with the lending institution.

• In making short-term investments, management may be advised to conduct transactions through one or two sources rather than consistently shopping the market for the highest rates on negotiable instruments. By building long-term relationships, small firms may gain access to sophisticated investment advice. A single informed suggestion may outweigh many times over the advantage of a slightly higher yield.

44

Small Business: Spotting the Buy Signs

I F it's true that "every problem is an opportunity in disguise," then many small companies put on the auction block by their owner may actually be good buys for astute investors.

This contrarian philosophy is expounded by a diverse group of investment professionals—Wall Street bankers, CPAs, entrepreneurs, and business brokers—who share a common conviction: Mixed in with the thousands of hopeless small companies now up for sale, there are hundreds of undiscovered gems. Most suffer for want of capital but are otherwise fiscally sound and blessed with good products in growth markets. Buyers with a bit of cash to invest can walk away with a steal.

"No doubt, this is one of the best times to shop for a small business," says a CPA active in mergers and acquisitions. "Many privately held companies that have been growing rapidly and in better times would have gone public have been frustrated by the drought in public financings. They've had no alternative but to sell. These companies make for exceptional buys. All they're lacking is capital."

Not to say that every business up for bids is a diamond in the rough. Many are outright losers, sponges that simply soak up the buyer's cash, time, talent, and resources. Selecting the ideal small business demands an insight into the many variables that make for a quality company and for a profitable business investment. Savvy buyers will consider the risks, the value, the projected return, and the available financing.

Experts make the following recommendations:

• Explore the strategy of "bootstrap acquisitions." It can cut a company's purchase price, reduce the amount of required financing and provide the seller with tax benefits. A gem that at first glance seems to be too costly to acquire may, through this approach, come quickly within the buyer's budget.

Assume ABC Company has $60,000 in fixed assets, $30,000 in cash, and $10,000 in goodwill. It's worth $100,000 but the prospective purchaser cannot afford to pay that much. To get around this obstacle, the seller draws the cash out of the business by having the firm redeem most of his shares. After this transaction, the company has a lower market value and the former owner's $30,000 is taxed as capital gains. Both parties benefit.

• Favor companies engaged in emerging markets over those active in mature industries. While the former may be more speculative, the trade-off of greater growth potential is often well worth the risk.

• Look for companies priced at their tangible book value.

"They may be exceptional bargains," says a partner with Touche Ross & Co., CPAs. "The tangible book value is determined by figuring assets less liabilities. If those assets have not been adjusted for inflation, they may be carried on the books at below-market prices. An office building purchased for $20,000 when the firm was founded, for example, and subsequently depreciated to an even lower figure, may have a current market value of $200,000. Adjusted tangible book value reflects the increase."

This "asset play" can make even money-losing firms attractive to those buyers who are aware of the hidden value. Some may want to buy the companies just to sell off the inflation-adjusted assets.

• Consider a "leveraged buyout." This financial magic act is ideally suited for tight credit, high interest periods. It enables small companies to acquire their competitors with little or no cash investment. The acquirer obtains credit to make the purchase simply by pledging the assets of the target firm.

It works like this. Company A learns that competitor B is pressed for cash and is up for sale. If B agrees, management of both firms contact a commercial finance company. Company A pledges B's assets to the finance company in return for a loan to acquire B. Typically, the finance company will lend up to 75 percent of company B's liquidation value. Assume Company B is on the market for $1 million and its property and receivables are valued at $1 million. Company A can get $750,000 or more just on the basis of B's assets. Best of all, Company A can repay the loan with Company B's profits. This is an excellent way for small companies to cash in on today's business bargains and to expand rapidly through highly leveraged acquisitions.

• Be wary of companies with outdated plant and equipment. Even if they are profitable, today's earnings may turn quickly to red ink when the company is forced to invest in new technology. Conversely, companies with state-of-the-art facilities are likely to be the most efficient producers and are in good position to increase market share.

• Pay special attention to poorly run companies that manage to earn a profit.

"Many of the companies we evaluate for our clients are sloppy, inefficient, and generally mismanaged but still in the black," says an executive with VR Financial Corp., investment bankers to small business. "I regard many of these outfits as real opportunities. They're making money even though the owners aren't capable managers. A talented entrepreneur can buy the venture for a bargain price, install operating improvements, and generate substantially improved profits. Soon after he takes control, the firm's value increases."

• Look favorably on companies that have some hedge against downside risk. Patented products, for example, provide protection from competitive attack and from the draining effects of price cutting.

"It is also a plus if the company is a market leader, even if the size of the market is relatively small," says George Naddaff, chairman of VR Business Brokers. "Dominant companies tend to have a strong advantage in gaining consumer loyalty and in achieving continued growth."

• Try to identify those franchise opportunities that are in the take-off stage. The idea is to find the McDonald's of tomorrow. Best bets are franchise operations with between 50 and 400 outlets. Most have passed through the shaky development stage, have demonstrated staying power but have not yet peaked in per unit sales or purchase terms. It is still possible to get in at a bargain price.

Still interested in buying a business? The rest is up to you. Ask accountants, attorneys, business brokers, and the Small Business Administration for leads. Study all the angles, basing your purchase decision on experience, audited financial reports, and intuition. Keep in mind that in one way, buying a business is much like running one: it's part art and part science.

45

Small Business: Spotting the Sell Signs

ASK the brightest minds on Wall Street how to profit in the stock market and many will answer that what counts is not what you buy but *when you sell*. Timing, as the saying goes, is everything. A hot issue held too long or a rising star sold short are opportunities lost to greed or impatience. Opportunities lost forever.

Good timing—a skillful blend of instinct and research—is also crucial when selling a small business. Much like shares of stock, companies move in and out of fashion, up and down the earnings curve. It is best to sell when all the positive signs converge at a single point in time.

"One of my clients, a self-made man, started a company that grew substantially over the years," says Herbert C. Speiser, a partner with the small-business practice of Touche Ross & Co., CPAs.

"The entrepreneur enjoyed a substantial income and had the security of knowing his firm could sell for a hefty price. So when he started getting on in age, and when it looked as if there'd be some serious business problems ahead, I suggested that he sell out. It's safe to say that he would have cleared several million dollars.

"But as happens all too often with company founders, he let emotions be his guide. Stubbornly—as a matter of pride—he decided to stay on just to prove he could face the problems and score another victory in his business career. But there was to be no happy ending. For a variety of reasons, business conditions worsened steadily and the company deteriorated before his eyes. I kept telling him to sell and he kept fighting against it. Now it's too late for him to change his mind. I doubt he could get any money for the firm.

"The message here, from my standpoint, is that if you think your company has earned in a given year more than it will likely earn at any other time in the future, it may be the time to sell. The goal is to sell from a position of strength, and strong earnings certainly provide that."

Another important consideration is the company's appeal, or lack of it, as a fashionable business. As the economy evolves, as consumer tastes move in one direction or another, certain types of companies emerge as hot prospects everyone wants to own.

"This is happening now with men's clothing stores," says the president of a retail consulting firm. "Some years ago, traditional men's shops were attractive businesses commanding substantial prices on the open market. Now, you can't give them away. Instead, discount clothing stores are the rage. Clearly, the idea is to sell when your business is in vogue. It's the old strike-while-the-iron-is-hot strategy."

Experts in accounting, marketing, and business brokerage offer the following guidelines for selling small businesses:

• Mature companies saddled with obsolete equipment must replace capital assets if the firm is to remain competitive. But this requires substantial investments. Machinery purchased ten years ago for $100,000 may now cost a half million dollars or more to replace. Inflation and technological advances account for the difference.

"But the investment in new equipment, which will likely require substantial borrowing, may knock out the company's profits," Speiser adds. "Expenses will rise and competitive forces may prevent management from boosting prices to compensate for this. The firm is caught in a squeeze. This may be a good time to sell out or to merge with a larger corporation that can better afford the investment."

• The need to refinance a long-term debt at sharply higher interest rates may also be viewed as a sell sign. Refinancing a debt balloon at 15 percent versus the old rate of 7 percent may cause fiscal shock waves that the company cannot absorb. Again, profits may shrink or even disappear and competition may block a price increase that would ease the pressure.

• Company owner-managers nearing retirement may want to sell out before age sixty-five if there are no capable successors to take over the reins. By delegating control to inexperienced employees, the owner's retirement benefits and long-term equity may be jeopardized. New management may run the firm into the ground. By the time the owner decides to sell, the company may be drained of its market value. A once-promising venture is seen as a loser.

• In most cases, once management decides to sell, the top priority is to put the firm in good operating condition. This means taking immediate action to cut spending and to extract the highest short-term profits. Accountants should be called in to straighten out the books and to use every legal technique to improve the company's numbers. This may help to bring a higher selling price.

• Although there are many ways to price a business that is up for sale—and here again it is a good idea to consult with an accountant—one rule of thumb is to add increments of one half of book value for every percentage point over 3 percent that the firm earns on sales. Using this formula, Company A earning 3 percent on sales is worth its book value; Company B earning 6 percent on sales may fetch several times its book value.

At the other end of the spectrum, companies operating in the minus column may be better liquidated than sold. Here, the corporation's assets—including inventory, equipment, real estate, and facilities—are sold to the highest bidders. Professional liquidators specialize in conducting these transactions.

"We are often asked to sell companies that, on close inspection, turn out to be candidates for liquidation," the retail consultant explains. "Troubled outfits, especially those in unpopular industries, fit into this category. It is not at all unusual to see a company that would bring $100,000 as a going concern actually bring $150,000 in a liquidation. Certainly the owner likes to have that extra $50,000.

"Another benefit of taking the liquidation approach is that payment is usually made in cash. Selling a company in fact may require the acceptance of notes. This involves some risk and may delay full payment for several years."

Deloitte Haskins & Sells, the national CPA firm, offers this simplified example for figuring the book and liquidation values of the hypothetical Elpmaxe company:

ELPMAXE CO.

Balance Sheet
December 31, 19X0 *(in 000s)*

	12/31/X0		12/31/X0
Current Assets	$3,380	Current Liabilities	$1,990
Fixed Assets	3,670	Long-Term Debt	3,055
		Total Liabilities	5,045
	————	Stockholders' Equity	2,005
Total Assets	$7,050	Total Liabilities and Stockholders' Equity	$7,050

ELPMAXE CO.

Methods of Valuation
"Balance-Sheet" Methods

	(000s)
I. Net Book Value	
Total Stockholders' Equity (represents assets net of liabilities) (Exhibit A)	$2,005
II. Adjusted Net Book Value	
Net Book Value (above)..............................	$2,005
Plus:	
Excess of appraised replacement value over book value of fixed assets (Note 1).....................	3,330
LIFO reserve (Note 2).............................	500
Value of patents not on books......................	50
Adjusted Net Book Value	$5,885

III. Liquidation Value

Net Book Value (above) $2,005
Plus:
   Excess of appraised liquidation value over book
     value of fixed assets (Note 3) 2,430
Less:
   Deficit of appraised liquidation value over book
     value of inventory (Note 3) .... (100)
   Income taxes due upon liquidation (Note 4) .... (1,165)

Liquidation Value $3,170

NOTES

1. Appraiser's opinion of cost to purchase assets of similar age and condition at their present retail value.

2. Inventories are carried at LIFO value, which is below their current cost. The present owners adopted LIFO in order to reduce income taxes.

3. Appraiser's opinion of value if fixed assets and inventory were to be sold in bulk at a forced sale.

4. Represents income taxes to be paid* if assets and liabilities were liquidated according to the above values.

---

*Based for purposes of simplicity, on an assumed rate of 50 percent. Actual tax will likely be lower due to capital gains considerations.

    The advantage of using book value as a reference point for computing the selling price is that the numbers are readily available. But book value may not reflect the fair market value of assets and liabilities. Patents, trademarks, and physical assets may be undervalued. An office building purchased twenty-five years ago for $100,000 and still carried on the books for that amount may be worth $1 million today.

    "Book value alone should never be used as the basis for selling a business," says a partner for Deloitte Haskins & Sells. "It is a typical buyer ploy to say 'Your book value is $2.5 million and that's what I want to pay for the firm.' But the seller must recognize that some of the assets may be undervalued. One sound approach is to adjust the book value to reflect current values and to contact a trade association to determine at what multiple of book value companies in your industry typically sell for."

• Be wary of payment plans based solely on shares of stock in another corporation. Unless the acquiring firm is publicly traded on a major stock exchange, the value of its shares may be difficult to establish. Even if the value is readily discernible, it is subject to rapid change. A sudden decline in sales may cause the stock price to plummet. Sellers taking stock as payment must be aware of the risks.

"Sometimes sellers take whatever terms they are offered because they want out of the business at any cost," the retail consultant adds. "Why? Because they think the company is going down the tubes and that there's no way to reverse its fate. But they may be wrong. I've seen many companies turned around simply by repositioning the business, bringing in a new partner, or obtaining additional financing. Saving the business this way is often more rewarding—both financially and psychologically—than selling it."

46

How to Hold On to Corporate Cash

YES, there can be too much of a good thing. Just ask the small business that finds itself blessed with a cache of record profits. The good news on the balance sheet may spell trouble with Uncle Sam. But there are ways to keep the spoils and stay within the law.

Call it corporate reserves or rainy day cash, to the government it's accumulated earnings subject to a punitive tax. The penalty applies when management retains, rather than distributes to shareholders, earnings in excess of an amount deemed reasonable to run the business. The charge is that the profits are being retained to avoid the tax on dividends.

"The Internal Revenue Service presumes there is a tax avoidance purpose subject to penalty for any taxable year in which earnings and profits accumulate beyond the reasonable needs of the business," says a tax partner with Price Waterhouse, CPAs.

"Because the government is scrutinizing corporate tax returns more closely than ever, it is incumbent on small business to formulate plans and to develop documentation to support a defense against IRS assertions regarding the accumulated earnings tax."

The tax, which can impede the small company's ability to retain capital for growth and expansion, is 27½ percent of the first $100,000 of "accumulated taxable income" and 38½ percent of the balance. Accumulated taxable income is defined as the corporation's taxable income for the year in question with certain adjustments, less the sum of dividends paid and the accumulated earnings credit. Corporations are entitled to an aggregate lifetime accumulation of $250,000 ($150,000 for service firms). Credits against this can be taken until the maximum is achieved.

"For example, assume Company ABC has taxable income of $300,000," the tax partner explains. "If it pays regular income tax of $118,000 plus dividends of $50,000, the $132,000 remaining is the accumulated taxable income, subject to a penalty tax of $39,790. This assumes the company exceeded the $250,000 credit in prior years and cannot justify any part of the $132,000 in the current year."

IRS examiners view the following as indicators of accumulated earnings:

- A high proportion of net liquid assets.
- A high working-capital ratio not justified by business requirements.
- No dividends paid or no consistent dividends policy.
- Loans to shareholders or other persons which have no business purpose.

Small-business owners can effectively challenge IRS presumptions and thus retain a greater percentage of earnings by demonstrating that the accumulated capital is required to meet the reasonable needs of the business. These strategies may be used to support management's position:

• The need to maintain adequate working capital through the company's operating cycles. These are the periods of time required to convert cash into raw materials, into finished products, into sales and accounts receivable and back to cash. Using the so-called Bardahl formula, familiar to accountants, may help to justify a specific amount of earnings necessary for working capital.

• Prove that accumulated earnings are slated for business expansion projects, such as the construction of a new store or branch office, and the money may not be subject to the penalty tax. This provision can enable small business to finance its growth internally, thus freeing management from dependence on outside lenders and investors. It can help to keep the company competitive.

47

Cash Management Makes Your Money Work Harder

MONEY moves through small business like sand through an hourglass. No sooner is it earned than it slips away to bankers, bill collectors, and the Internal Revenue Service. Credits turn quickly to debits.

Cash management can slow this process, giving companies extended use of and extra earnings from their money. It does so, in part, by replacing the open-ended flow of dollars and cents with a carefully controlled program of short-term investments and planned disbursements.

"Cash management looks at the company's funds as a source of income rather than simply as a means of paying bills," says a consulting services partner for Main Hurdman, CPAs. "It seeks to retain funds for as long as possible, to put them to work making more money and to bring these incremental earnings down to the bottom line."

The Main Hurdman partner, a former banker, recommends that companies "open zero-balance accounts. Rather than letting cash sit idle in standard accounts, the zero-balance option allows the company to fund the account only when a check is drawn against it. The company knows when it is sending out checks but not when they will be presented to the bank for payment. Zero-balance lets management retain use of its funds until that time.

"There is generally a fee for this but it may be considerably less than the amount the firm can earn by investing the money until it is needed. As a sweetener, the zero-balance fees may be negotiated away as part of an overall banking relationship, especially if the firm maintains some funded accounts with the bank."

The high cost of borrowing as well as the attractive yields on invested capital have brought a new emphasis on cash management. Consider these additional strategies:

• Pay local vendors through remote disbursements. Put simply, this involves opening a secondary bank account in another state, preferably a remote location. By paying substantial bills through the account, the firm picks up several days of float. It can take that long for the vendor's bank to collect the funds. Over the course of a year, this can add up to thousands of dollars.

"Big business has been doing this for years," says a manager with the national accounting firm of Touche Ross. "There's no reason small business shouldn't make use of this technique, especially for big payments to major vendors. Although the Federal Reserve Board doesn't like the practice, it is permissible."

• Small firms active in the export market, even on a limited basis, may be wise to open accounts in U.S. branches of foreign banks.

"Let's say a small company does business with a Canadian account," the Main Hurdman partner explains. "Checks from the foreign customer may be treated as non-cash items, meaning they may not clear for up to a month. But if management opens an account with a stateside branch of a Canadian bank, the checks can clear in a few days. If the money is invested, this could produce $500 or more in interest on a $50,000 payment."

• Look closely at bank-sponsored cash management plans. These are sold to commercial depositors for a fee. But beware—the bank's best interests may conflict with those of the small company. The plans are designed principally to keep most of the firm's accounts with the bank.

The best approach is to seek the advice of an accountant or an independent consultant in reviewing cash management options. They can point out the widest range of alternatives and can advise on their impact on the firm's operations.

48

How to Get Listed on the Stock Exchange

ASK a small business if it's ready for a listing on the stock exchange and you'll probably be dismissed as a fool. Management thinks of Big Board names like Ford and Exxon and knows it's light-years away from that crowd. The stock exchange seems like a club for the multinational giants.

Well, not exactly. While the New York Stock Exchange may boast the bluest of blue chip pedigrees, it is not the only show in town. The American Stock Exchange and the over-the-counter market are home to thousands of small- and medium-sized businesses and the welcome mat is out to others seeking to join. Even the smallest public companies can qualify for a stock exchange listing and many can use this as a vehicle for rapid growth.

Stock market listings can help to establish clear market values, to attract investors, and to open the faucets of capital. What's more, nothing else so clearly announces that a business has arrived and is ready to take its place in the big leagues.

"We obtained an over-the-counter listing at the time of our first public offering in 1971," says the treasurer of a firm which fabricates and installs construction products. "Our sales were then $8.7 million annually. The best proof of our dramatic growth with the over-the-counter listing is that 10 years later our sales had climbed to $135 million. The listing has given us an excellent source of periodic financing."

By listing with the National Association of Securities Dealers Automated Quotation system (NASDAQ), over-the-counter stocks can gain the attention and visibility generally accorded only to the corporate giants.

"Our computerized market, the NASDAQ system, was formed to bring liquidity and credibility to over-the-counter stock transactions," says Gordon S. Macklin, president of the National Association of Securities Dealers. "It links a network of brokers across the nation. Every quotation change of a NASDAQ-listed stock is reported into the system the moment it occurs. By checking computer terminals, brokers can give investors up-to-the-minute price information."

A NASDAQ listing can aid small public companies seeking to build a greater following for their stock. The major benefits include the following:

• Exposure. Current NASDAQ quotes are carried on more than 80,000 broker terminals around the world. Investors can get breaking price information on NASDAQ companies whether they are in a broker's office in Paris or in Pittsburgh. In addition, NASDAQ trading activities are published daily in many newspapers and financial publications. This focuses investor attention on a select group of over-the-counter companies.

• Liquidity. Dealers of NASDAQ-listed stocks are required to continuously post bid and asked prices, thus assuring liquidity for all the shares. This can help business owners and investors sell their interests at market value.

• Broker supports. Market makers in NASDAQ issues are likely to promote the shares by committing research and sales efforts to them. Investors learn that even the smallest companies make for good investments.

To be eligible for a NASDAQ listing, companies must be registered with the Securities and Exchange Commission as 12-G public corporations, must have assets of at least $2 million, capital and surplus of $1 million, 100,000 shares held by non-management, 300 stockholders of record, and at least two brokers willing to make a market in the stock.

NASDAQ entry fees are based on the number of shares outstanding and range from $1,000 to $5,000; add to this annual fees of from $250 to $2,500. Companies interested in exploring NASDAQ participation may contact Gordon Macklin at the National Association of Securities Dealers, 1735 K Street, Washington, DC 20006.

Many major companies are listed on the NASDAQ. Names like Coors, U.S. Trust, and Hoover share billing with the small businesses that make up the bulk of NASDAQ's roughly 3,400 companies.

"There is great prestige to be in the market with some of America's leading companies," Macklin adds. "That can propel a once-obscure firm into the business spotlight."

Still, a NASDAQ listing is not recommended for every company. Many entrepreneurs are uncomfortable with the higher levels of public exposure, the volatility of stock prices, and the scrutiny of security analysts. They may prefer to be privately owned or to be traded over-the-

counter without a central market listing. It is best to review
the alternatives with investment bankers and accountants.

Some companies prefer what they consider to be the
greater prestige and visibility of a listing on the American
Stock Exchange. Many emerging firms seek their first stock
market listing on the Amex; others switch over after getting
their feet wet over-the-counter.

Established in 1849, the Amex has for years been the
also-ran to the mammoth New York Stock Exchange. It
trades in far fewer issues than the Big Board and its shares
have a much smaller market value. But important to the
management of emerging companies is that the Amex has
always been closely associated with small- and medium-
sized businesses.

An Amex vice-president puts it this way: "We like to
think of the ideal new listing candidates as threshold
companies. By this, we mean those that are rapidly
expanding and are about to cross the boundaries from
emerging growth to a more mature stage. We are deeply
involved with these firms not only through their listings on
the Amex but also through our increasing efforts to
represent growth businesses in the nation's capital."

Like NASDAQ, the Amex is not limited to small
companies. Emerging firms that do gain a listing there will
find themselves sharing company with some of the most
venerable names in corporate America. Many believe this
association can only bring them greater status and prestige.

American Stock Exchange listing requirements include
the following:

• The company must be publicly held with at least
500,000 shares outstanding.

• The market value of the shares must be at least
$3 million.

- There must be at least 1,000 stockholders.
- Net income of the last fiscal year must be a minimum of $400,000 and net tangible assets must total $4 million.

The Amex initial listing fee is $15,000 plus one cent per share for the first 2 million shares, one half cent per share for the second 2 million shares, one quarter cent per share for the next 6 million shares, and one eighth cent per share for the balance. Once a company is listed, annual fees, which are also based on the number of outstanding shares, range from $3,500 to $10,000.

Public companies that choose to list are faced with some new requirements. The Amex demands, for example, that companies have outside representation on their board of directors. For this and other reasons, not every company that has won a listing has been pleased with the experience. A small number of firms choose to reverse their original decision and remove the listing. Those small companies that take this action usually feel lost in the shuffle or are unable to attract investor interest.

One way around the exposure problem is to combine a stock exchange listing with a public relations campaign designed to draw media attention to the company and its activities. Those entrepreneurs who generate a sense of excitement about their ventures will attract investors, boost the stock price, and greatly improve the financing environment.

The best bet is to review the options for stock market listings with a team of company advisers including consultants and the experts in law, accounting, and promotion. Pick their brains and then make a decision.

49

Turn Vacant Space into a Profit Center

AFTER years of sending money to Uncle Sam, why not reverse the balance of payments in your favor? Do it by leasing space to the federal government. Turn a part of your plant, office, or warehouse into an unexpected profit center.

Unbeknownst to most small companies, the U.S. government turns to private enterprise for some of its workspace requirements. Any business with excess or underutilized space—from a room to a warehouse—can participate in the General Services Administration's leasing program.

"We are responsible for providing workspace for more than three quarters of a million federal workers in all fifty states," says a senior official with the GSA's leasing division. "Most federal agencies, except the Departments of Agriculture, Commerce, and Defense, and the U.S. Postal Service, ask our office to lease facilities when they need additional space. Small firms can profit by participating in the program."

It works like this:

• When a federal agency needs room to expand in a given city or state, it provides the nearest GSA regional office with a detailed description of its space requirements, including square footage, number of employees to be housed, and technical features such as specially equipped computer rooms.

• GSA officials review the request for compliance with all government regulations. If the green light is flashed, they try to fill the space request from the current inventory of federally controlled facilities. A search is conducted of government-owned and leased properties with an eye toward filling vacancies and making more efficient use of available workspace.

• Should this fail to turn up adequate facilities, the GSA taps a variety of sources in the private real estate market.

"One of the first steps is to check our mailing lists of private property owners and managers," the GSA official adds. "These are sources who keep us abreast of the real estate they have available for lease. Should we find something that matches our needs, we work with the parties to try to negotiate a deal.

"Any company with space to rent can get on our mailing list by submitting the appropriate form to the GSA. Full details may be obtained by writing the Leasing Division, Office of Space Management, GSA, Washington, DC 20405."

Solicitations are also made through newspaper advertising and real estate brokers. Although the GSA will not pay brokerage commissions, property owners can compensate bona fide real estate brokers for arranging government lease transactions.

GSA leases are negotiated on a free market basis. Most leases run from three to five years but they can extend up to twenty. Lease rates are established by comparing various offers, reviewing local market factors, and studying comparable transactions in the region. Where several property owners are vying for a federal lease, the GSA will often play one against another in an effort to win the lowest rate.

But cost alone is not the only determinant in awarding lease contracts. Property owners must comply with a laundry list of federal regulations. Those who come closest to meeting all government rules have the best chance of closing a deal.

For example, in the case of two similar properties with similar lease rates, the GSA is obliged to favor the one that meets more of the government's handicap accessibility features. Details on all federal requirements are listed in bid solicitation forms available from the GSA.

One lessor, who prefers to remain anonymous, leases 11,000 square feet of space to two federal agencies.

"You do have to put up with some red tape but it's worth it. I am satisfied with the program and with the fact that it can be profitable to do business with the federal government."

50

How to Protect Your "Better Ideas"

IN small business, outthinking the competition is still the best way to pole-vault to the top. But management must act swiftly to protect its better ideas from widespread imitation. That's the only way to keep the advantage.

Three major types of protection—patents, trademarks, and trade secrets—can shield proprietary information from competitive use. Each is effective in guarding a different aspect of a company's assets and operations. Prudent business owners will identify potential risks, determine the best form of protection, and crack down on violators.

Experts suggest the following:

• Trade secrets are attractive because they can protect virtually every type of business information. Customer lists, computer programs, recipes, processes, formulas, and manufacturing techniques can receive trade secret protection without formal application to government agencies.

"A company's private information automatically qualifies for trade secret status if management does its best to keep the information from getting to potential competitors," says a lawyer specializing in the field. "As a trade secret, it is protected from competitive use. Should another company wrongfully obtain the information, it can be prevented from profiting from it."

A partner with a law firm offers this example. "Take the case of a company with a secret recipe for making a certain type of food. If the firm keeps the recipe under lock and key, reveals it only to those employees with a need to know, and requires them to sign a confidentiality agreement, the recipe will likely be considered a trade secret. If a competitor manages to seize a copy of the recipe, it can be stopped from marketing another food product based on it."

But there is a chink in the trade secret armor: it does not protect against independent development of the same commercial idea, innovation, or device. Competitors coming up with an identical recipe without having access to the original may be free to use it.

• Patents provide more formal and exclusive protection but are granted only for inventions. Issued by the U.S. Patent Office after a lengthy application process that can take two years or more, patents grant sole rights to make or sell inventions. Should a competitor independently develop the same product, it can be enjoined from making use of it.

But patents have their weak links too. Most important, they expire in seventeen years, at which time competitors may produce and market identical products. Trade secrets, on the other hand, provide indefinite protection. The formula for Coca-Cola has been around for more than 100 years.

"Certainly, patents are not always the best way to protect business secrets," the law firm partner adds. "Patent applications demand a full description of the invention. Once this is in the public domain, competitors may find ways to produce similar but not identical products that do not infringe on the patent. That's a risk you have to be willing to take."

• Trademarks protect a company's promotional symbols, including brand names, advertising phrases, and product designs.

To claim ownership of a trademark, the firm must first use it in marketing goods or services. Management then applies to the Patent Office for exclusive rights. Providing the trademark, or one closely resembling it, has not been previously registered, rights will be granted. The trademark owner can prevent others from using the same symbol.

Companies investing time and money in developing innovative products and practices should make certain to give them the very best protection. Work with an attorney experienced in this legal specialty.

51

New Products: Smaller Can Be Better

FROM the paper cup to the pocket calculator, successful new products have scored in the marketplace by finding a void and filling it. Enlightened entrepreneurs have prospered by outmaneuvering rather than overpowering established forces.

The formula still applies today. Small companies seeking to put their stamp on the commercial landscape by bringing new products or services to market are advised to sidestep head-to-head confrontation with corporate giants, relying instead on flexibility and creativity to build sales.

"Small firms think that their size is an impediment to marketing new products, but it can, in fact, be a strength," says Harvey Moskowitz, a partner with the national CPA firm of Seidman & Seidman. "What they lack in resources they can compensate for with speed and innovation. When an opportunity arises, a small business can often get a product on the shelves while the big corporation is still holding meetings on the subject."

Adds a new-product specialist at the consulting firm of Arthur D. Little: "Because they must work with enormous volumes, major corporations will often ignore market segments that can be extremely profitable for smaller firms. By identifying these niches and aggressively pursuing them, management can achieve significant expansion without going one-on-one against dominating competitors."

Marketing consultants offer the following guidelines for filling the gaps in brand-name product lines:

• Focus on industries or product categories that thrive on innovation rather than a stable technology. In this environment, a brand name and marketing efficiency may be of secondary importance to a technical breakthrough or an updated product feature. A small firm with a hot new patent may outsell established competitors.

"There is also a financial advantage in this type of market," the Little consultant adds. "In a mature industry like the water heater business, there is little difference among competing products and they are priced at, say, cost plus 10 percent. That slim margin makes it difficult for emerging ventures to justify the capital investment necessary to enter the business. But in a creative industry, such as medical devices, a proprietary product can be priced at three or five times cost."

• Favor those products that call for low-volume, high-priced sales. This approach, which is generally labor intensive rather than capital intensive, allows for a faster and less costly entry into the market. Management can start up and expand with minimum financing. Target industries include computer software and robotics, both of which also stress the creative element.

"One of my clients makes heat exchangers, but rather than mass producing them, as is the norm, this firm specializes in custom-made units," Moskowitz says. "The number of units it markets, considered a meager volume by major manufacturers, is more than enough to yield a substantial profit."

• Look for weaknesses in successful products now on the market. Produce imitations free of the defects and promote the competitive advantage. Providing there are no patent infringements, this short-cuts the development process, eliminating substantial costs.

"This need not be a highly technical change," says another Arthur D. Little consultant. "One small company we worked with revolutionized the paper cup industry when it simply added a plastic coating to the inside of the standard cup. Until then, hot beverages soaked through the cardboard, rendering the cups ineffective. This fundamental improvement made for a highly successful product and led to the company's purchase by a major corporation."

Experts advise steering clear of highly regulated products or industries. Government regulations covering design, manufacturing, and safety features may subject the products to excessive costs and law suits.

52

Mailing Lists Make Profitable Side Business

SMALL companies searching for new sources of income may find they can profit twice on every sale: first by marketing products or services and then by renting the customers' names. The strategy can build a lucrative side business, bringing up to $100,000 or more to the bottom line.

"Virtually every business has a valuable asset in the form of its customer names," says an executive of the Kleid Co., mailing list consultants. "Other companies selling similar or related products view the names as valuable sales leads and are therefore willing to pay handsomely for their use. By putting the names into list form and having them professionally marketed, the company can rent them for from $40 to $80 per thousand.

"Take a company that sells video equipment. Its customer names are sought after by direct-mail marketers selling peripheral equipment, video magazines, video tapes, and other types of home entertainment products.

Once news of these lists reaches the direct-mail industry, a wide cross section of marketers may come forward to rent them.

"This can produce a windfall for the list owner. A modest-sized list of 25,000 names can bring in upward of $100,000 a year, and a good 50,000-name list can earn more than $500,000 annually."

Direct-mail specialists, known as list brokers, assist companies in computerizing their lists and in marketing them to prospective users. In return for 20 percent of the gross rentals, brokers promote the lists in industry publications, negotiate rental agreements, and do the billing. Acting in a similar capacity to real estate agents, list brokers circulate news of the list's availability and generally split the commission on a 50/50 basis should another broker be involved in the transaction.

"Clients have the option of granting the list broker an exclusive or registering it with any number of brokers simultaneously," the Kleid executive explains. "There are two schools of thought on this. Some believe that by giving the broker an exclusive—and thereby assuring him of a co-broker's fee even if another broker makes the deal—he will have the incentive to properly promote and publicize the list. But others contend that by refusing to grant exclusivity, they keep all the list brokers equally motivated to market the list."

"Hot lists"—those in most demand for direct-mail promotions—are heavily weighted with customers who have made purchases within the past year. Typically, a mail order firm will test a sample of the list, 5,000 to 10,000 names, basing the decision for further use on the test results. Should the mailing prove successful, the marketer will likely work his way through the entire list.

Although the general rule holds that marketable lists must have a minimum of 25,000 names, there are exceptions.

Small firms with highly specialized customer lists may achieve successful list rentals with as few as 2,000 names. Customers using certain types of sophisticated computers, for example, are promising contacts for marketers of compatible software. They may be willing to conduct small mailings to reach key market segments.

Companies marketing customer names retain ownership of the lists and simply rent them for one-time use only. Direct marketers must gain the owner's permission and must pay the rental fee for each use. Lists are seeded with control names, often the owner's staff members, to monitor unauthorized mailings.

One caveat is to make certain that the lists are rented to reputable businesses whose products do not compete with the list owner's. Experts suggest examining the promotional literature and running a check on the direct-mail company before agreeing to the rental. It is also important to honor the requests of those customers who ask that their names not be released to third parties.

"Renting customer names can make for a profitable side business but it's important to remember that there are many, many lists competing in the marketplace," says the president of a mail order house. "To be successful, yours must be a good list handled by a good broker."

Names of list brokers may be obtained from advertising agencies or from the Direct Mail Marketing Association, 6 East 43rd Street, New York, NY 10017.

53

Agency Helps Business Tap Fastest-Growing Markets

T UCKED away in a quiet corner of the federal bureaucracy, a little-known government agency is helping small business gain access to the world's fastest-growing markets. By financing and insuring high risk foreign investments, the Overseas Private Investment Corporation makes multinationals of companies a fraction of the size of the Fortune 500.

Lured by the prospect of ground-floor business opportunities in Asia, Africa, and the Middle East, small businesses are opening offices, warehouses, and manufacturing plants there. But others—equally confident of the commercial prospects—stay away from what they perceive as political and social risks. In nations racked by wars and instability, they fear that their assets will be damaged or nationalized.

"It's our mission to insure against these perils and to provide general financial assistance for American companies seeking to invest in developing nations," says an OPIC spokesman. "About 30 percent of our resources are directed at small business and we expect this figure to rise as entrepreneurs become more aware of the explosive opportunities in emerging nations. In 1969, for example, U.S. trade to developing countries totaled $11 billion; last year the volume soared to $87 billion."

The OPIC offers three major services:

• The agency's political-risk policies provide insurance against currency inconvertibility (the inability to take dollars out of the foreign country), nationalization, and physical damage to business assets resulting from war, revolution, insurrection, or civil strife.

Insurance premiums—written for up to twenty-year fixed-rate periods—are 1.5 percent of the amount of the insured investment. This covers all three risk components; individual components may be purchased at lower rates. The handful of private insurers selling political-risk coverage rarely commit to long-term rates and are often substantially more expensive in the most turbulent markets.

• OPIC's foreign investment financing program makes extended-term loans (seven to twelve years) of up to $4 million for small businesses establishing commercial interests in developing nations. Although the loans are made at bank-equivalent interest rates, the program is important because small firms are often unable to secure private financing for high-risk foreign investments.

• Partial funding of feasibility studies, to a maximum of $100,000, is available to companies exploring the opportunities in third-world investments.

"Assume the management of a small U.S. company likes the idea of opening a distributorship in India but wants to first take a close look at the labor pool, the costs of real estate, the market for its products," the OPIC spokesman explains. "Our feasibility funding can provide them with 60 percent of the money they'll need for travel, business studies, and related expenses.

"If the project goes ahead, the funding is repayable within two years or it may be applied toward insurance premiums. If the firm decides against making the overseas investment, the funds need not be paid back."

OPIC programs are limited to investments made in an agency-approved list of more than 100 countries, most of which have a per capita gross national product of less than $2,950. Companies interested in tapping OPIC's services must submit an application detailing sales, management, credit, and product information. Applications are judged according to established lending and underwriting standards. Details are available by writing to OPIC, 1129 20th St. NW, Washington, DC 20527.

"OPIC facilitated our entry into Haiti," says the president of a paper company. "With their $1.25 million financing package, we opened a plant to serve the local corrugated box industry. We have found this to be an extremely rewarding market and one—thanks to the insurance coverage—with acceptable risks."

54

Cashing In on Business Real Estate

B ENEATH the products, the logo, and the goodwill, small business has a hidden asset that can generate thousands of dollars of extra income. This source of cash is the company's real estate.

Raw land, factories, warehouses, and office space—often depreciated and carried on a company's books at a fraction of market value—can be broken out from the business and developed into separate profit centers. The goal is to capitalize on some of the company's most valuable assets.

"Because most small firms rarely look at their real estate as income-producing assets, they fail to tap the earning power it represents," says a vice-president of Security Pacific Realty Advisory Services, a bank consulting group active in real estate. "But major corporations have been implementing strategies to make the most of their property for years and small business can do the same.

There are countless ways to profit from real estate assets
without changing the nature of the business."

Experts recommend the following:

• "Companies with excess work, storage, or production space may consolidate operations into a segment of
their facilities, leasing the ideal footage to one or more corporate tenants. Professional workplace analyses, prepared
by architects or interior designers, can help most firms
reduce their space requirements.

The Security Pacific executive notes: "Should consoli-
dation eliminate the need for an ancillary facility, management can subdivide this property into so-called incubator
units. These are small work areas especially designed for
use by emerging companies as showrooms, light manufacturing plants, or distribution centers.

"Because these modest-sized units typically claim the
highest rentals, the incubators can produce substantial
income. What's more, once the properties are performing
as income-producers, they can be sold to investors. Well-
situated facilities with quality tenants can claim sales prices
of ten times their income stream. An office building
generating rents of $100,000 a year may sell for as much as
$1 million."

• Through the technique of sale-leasebacks, the
business may intentionally change roles from property
owner to tenant. By selling its facilities to an investor—and
leasing them back on a long-term basis—the company
obtains a lump sum cash payment while retaining use of the
facility. Although the firm assumes an additional expense in
the form of rent, it also secures capital that can be used to
expand its business and bolster profits. Investment bankers
and real estate brokers can help to arrange sale-leasebacks.

• Property currently used for manufacturing or storage may be rezoned or remarketed for more productive utilization.

"An area changing from industrial to office or retail use will likely experience a surge in property values and market rentals," the executive explains. "Owners may be wise to adapt their facilities to this higher use even if this mandates moving the business to an alternate location and selling or leasing the property to others."

• Owners selling their companies or subsidiaries may do well to conduct two separate sales: one for the going business and one for its real estate. For example, an investor seeking a 20 percent pretax return on his investment may be willing to spend $500,000 to acquire a business with a pretax profit of $100,000.

"But before selling it for that amount, the owner could sell the real estate for $200,000, creating a sale-leaseback whereby the firm rents the facility for $200,000 a year," says a Security Pacific senior officer.

"Because this cuts the company's bottom line to $80,000, the investor seeking the 20 percent return will not only pay $400,000 for the business. But because the seller has already collected $200,000 on the property sale, he is ahead by $100,000."

It is best to structure all real estate transactions within the context of the company's total financial planning.

55

The Price Is Right

PUTTING the right price tag on business products
and services can make the difference between robust
sales and no sales at all. The goal is to strike a delicate
balance between the company's need to profit and the
consumer's search for value.

Savvy pricing strategies are especially important for
small business. Giant competitors in numerous industries
have used aggressive pricing to put small firms out of
business, only to raise prices once they control the market.
By viewing price as a competitive weapon, management
can beat the blue chips at their own game. What small
business lacks in size it can make up in speed and agility.

"Sharp pricing benefits every business from small
manufacturers to professional firms," says a partner with
Seidman & Seidman, CPAs. "Let's assume a choice account
is up for grabs on the basis of competitive bids. A company
that keeps track of its costs and bases prices on them can
shave margins to win the account and still remain

profitable. Management knows how far it can go to outmaneuver competitors."

Consider these pricing strategies:

• Start by establishing a price range within which you believe the product can be sold. The floor price is the minimum required to cover costs and maintain working capital. The ceiling—the maximum amount consumers will spend—varies with prevailing economic and competitive factors.

• Determine the ceiling price by conducting market research or by taking the "best-guess trial-and-error" approach. With the latter, management starts at the highest possible figure and then scales back at the first sign of consumer resistance or competitive pressure. This top-down strategy makes sense because it is generally easier to lower prices than to raise them.

• Monitor all costs on an ongoing basis. Sharp increases in raw materials, advertising, or interest rates may necessitate immediate price increases to protect profit margins. Conversely, a sudden drop in costs may create opportunities for aggressive pricing and related boosts in market share. Small firms that beat competitors in bringing lower prices to market may win and keep many new customers.

• Classify costs as either fixed or variable. Put simply, fixed costs remain constant regardless of the number of units produced. They include supervisors' salaries, plant rental, and property taxes. Variable costs, such as direct labor and raw materials, rise and fall with production volume.

"It is no longer acceptable for a company to determine its overall costs and to leave it at that," the Seidman partner adds. "In today's competitive and often inflationary environment, even the smallest firms must know their costs on an item-by-item basis. That's the only way to develop accurate pricing and to keep prices moving up and down in sync with market factors."

• Build intangibles into the selling price. When the elements of prestige, status, and pride come into play, extravagant prices may be an advantage. Here, the ideal price defies both logic and the market mechanism.

The story is told of the merchant saddled with a large inventory of private-brand perfume that would not budge from the shelves. Priced at $5 a bottle, it experienced dismal sales. Acting on a hunch, the retailer tripled the price and advertised the item as a premium fragrance sold only in his shop. It worked like a charm: the entire inventory sold out within two weeks.

• Ask smaller vendors for exclusive rights to sell their products in your market area. Peppering the merchandise line with exclusives provides more leeway in setting high ceiling prices and in protecting those prices from low-balling by corporate giants. The strategy insulates small business from damaging competition.

Establish a regular schedule for reviewing all prices with an eye toward keeping them in line with market conditions.

56
Franchising: How to Pick a Winner

FOR thousands of Americans, the road to self-employment dead-ends at the local hamburger haven. Lured by the promise of a "sure thing," they invest their life savings in a franchise said to be the next McDonald's. Instead, it turns out to be a candidate for bankruptcy.

Although there is still money to be made in franchising, the secret to success is selecting the right opportunity from the start. This means sorting out meaningful claims from pie in the sky. Because fledgling entrepreneurs rarely have the resources to buy into the best-known franchises—many of which are now reclaiming franchise units as company stores—they must pick and choose among less prominent names in the marketplace.

"For the business person whose personal characteristics are suited to franchising, the challenge is to find a reputable and profitable franchise at a reasonable price," says a vice-president of the Bank of America.

"Prospective buyers must locate the franchise opportunity that offers a good profit after operating expenses, debt obligations, and franchisor fees are paid. To determine whether a franchise opportunity represents a sound investment, the prospective franchisee must carefully evaluate the company, its record of success, and its franchise agreement. The key to a successful franchise business is investigation, investigation, investigation."

Lawyers, accountants, and government officials experienced in franchise operations make the following recommendations for conducting an informed search:

• Pay more attention to the quality of the franchise than the years it has been in business. The familiar warning to reject those franchise systems in operation for less than three years may cause investors to turn their backs on the most promising opportunities. Buying in before a franchise peaks can produce substantial returns on a relatively small investment.

• Demand a copy of the franchisor's disclosure statement. This document, which must be presented to the franchisee at least ten days before a contract is signed or a payment is made, provides revealing information on the franchisor's business experience and practices.

"Pay particular attention to the total investment required to obtain the franchise and the amount of continuing payments necessary to run it," says a franchise specialist with the Federal Trade Commission. "Prospective investors should make certain that they have enough capital to meet all obligations. Also, if the franchisor makes sales or profit projections, it must reveal in the disclosure statement the number and percentage of existing franchisees that have achieved or exceeded these results. Studying these figures is a good way to compare the franchisor's promises with its real-world performance.

"Another reliable indicator contained in the disclosure statement is the franchisor's litigation history. In other words, who is suing the firm? If fifty existing franchisees are bringing legal action against the franchisor, there is ample reason to be wary. Perhaps the franchisor is not delivering management or promotional services as called for in the franchise agreement."

• Check the franchisor's income statement to determine its revenues mix. If the lion's share of income is generated from franchise sales rather than from royalties paid by existing units, the system may be geared to attracting investors rather than helping them prosper.

• Seek references from current franchisees, both on the system's profitability and on their relationship with the franchisor's management. Do not ask the franchisor to set up these meetings. Make contact on your own.

"The most important caveat is never to let yourself be hustled," the FTC official adds. "Compare several franchise systems, call as many existing franchisees as you possibly can, and get professional assistance in reviewing the various offerings. Much like any other investment, franchising demands caution. Only fools will proceed without it."

57

Cash and Consulting Helps Bring Inventions to Market

FEW challenges in American business rival that of bringing inventions to market. Would-be Edisons must pass through a gauntlet of charlatans, skeptics, and rip-off artists lining the road to commercial success. But there are ways to detour around the obstacles, gaining objective appraisals and in some cases financial support.

One approach is through a unique invention clearing-house run by the international consulting firm of Arthur D. Little, Inc. Through its ADL Enterprises division, the firm provides a wide range of invention-related services designed to assist entrepreneurs developing new products, systems, and formulas.

"We welcome the opportunity to work with inventors for our mutual benefit," says an ADL vice-president. "We'll buy, sell, license, and finance inventions, find manufacturers to produce them, and even form new companies around promising products. If it has to do with inventions, there's a chance we'll be able to work with it in some way.

"Inventors who believe they are on to something promising are welcome to bring the innovation to our attention. Although a prototype or a working system is not necessary—we know many inventors don't have the financial resources to get to that stage single-handedly—we do insist on some strong evidence of the invention's feasibility. What's more, we are not interested in working with hobbyists producing new gadgets, like the latest improvement on the Christmas tree stand. Our emphasis is on technology-based inventions."

Qualified inventors may want to explore these ADL activities:

• Through its invention management program, ADL reviews innovative products and systems, selects those it considers especially promising, and provides the capital and consulting services required for further development. Typically, the firm will invest $50,000 (but this can go as high as $1 million) for technical work, market studies, cost analyses, and patent applications.

The ultimate goal is to license the technology to manufacturers in return for royalties on the products sold. In most cases, ADL Enterprises and the inventor share this royalty income on a 50/50 basis. ADL collects the money, audits the payments, and remits half to the inventor.

ADL reviews 800 innovations each year, selecting ten to fifteen for the management program.

• ADL's equity investment program provides capital to small high-technology companies in exchange for a maximum of 20 percent of the companies' stock.

"This is venture capital–type financing but with a twist," the V.P. explains. "In addition to investing development money, generally in the $200,000 to $400,000 range, we also provide intensive management consulting. The ventures we support can tap the expertise of Arthur Little's 1,400 professionals.

"The most likely candidates for this program are innovative companies in the earliest stages of development. ADL does not want to be passive investors—we'll contribute our talents and ideas—but we are not looking to dominate the companies either. Control will remain with current management."

The president of a small producer of communications products credits ADL with providing financial support and marketing expertise. "Arthur Little made a $200,000 investment in our firm and made available to us the services of their telecommunications staff. This has proven invaluable to our success in developing high technology products."

• Small companies seeking to market rather than develop inventions may find suitable ADL-produced technologies available for licensing. This can provide a low-cost entry into new and potentially profitable markets. Small firms have licensed the rights to a videotex terminal and a system for detecting toxic gases in the air. Royalties depend on the type of innovation and its application.

Companies and inventors interested in exploring ADL programs, or in submitting innovations for review, may write to ADL Enterprises, Acorn Park, Cambridge, MA 02140.

VI
FILLING IN THE GAPS

58

How Bankruptcy Can Help Troubled Firms

BANKRUPTCY—the most dreaded word in the business lexicon—can be a blessing in disguise. Creative use of the bankruptcy laws puts creditors at bay, voids prohibitive contracts, and generally helps troubled companies return to fiscal well-being.

Of the two classifications of business bankruptcy, Chapters 7 and 11, the former is a cut-and-dried route to commercial liquidation. The company's assets are distributed to the creditors in accordance with a statutory scheme. Chapter 7 is used principally when there is no chance for rehabilitation and there are insufficient assets to pay creditors' claims in full.

But Chapter 11, which contemplates a continuing business operation and a rehabilitation of the fiscally troubled firm, can serve as a management aid. The major benefit is that indebtedness in existence at the filing date is frozen until a payment plan is confirmed by the court. The company may move forward, temporarily protected from its creditors.

"The corporation actually continues as if it were a brand-new business," says a partner with Ballon, Stoll & Itzler, a law firm specializing in bankruptcy practice. "Just how and when the debt is eventually paid off is determined by a vote of the creditors.

"Negotiations are first conducted with a committee composed of the largest unsecured creditors. By skillfully negotiating with this group, the debtor can reduce its liability to a fraction of the original sum. In a typical transaction, a company recently settled with its creditors for 12.5 cents on the dollar. In effect, 87.5 percent of the debt was excused. When will creditors accept so small a settlement? When they are made to understand that the alternative, liquidation, will yield even less."

Just how a company fares in Chapter 11 depends, in part, on the imagination and negotiating skills of its legal counsel. Bankruptcy laws, while setting guidelines for structuring these settlements, do allow for creative strategies. The idea is to use the relief measures provided by Chapter 11 to help reverse a company's financial woes.

Reorganization specialists suggest the following strategies:

• Commercial tenants locked into prohibitive leases may use the bankruptcy laws as an escape hatch. Assume that a tenant's $10 per square foot rent is more than doubled by inflation escalators built into the lease. The higher rent may exceed the company's ability to pay.

"Fortunately, Chapter 11 provides for a legal way to void the lease," the lawyer explains. "By declaring bankruptcy, the company's liability is limited to a claim for one year's rent. This claim is treated like all other unsecured claims under the bankruptcy plan. In essence, the landlord may have to settle for pennies on the dollar. Most important, the tenant is free to relocate to more economical facilities.

"There is a corollary to this. A bankrupt company can actually make money on its lease. If its current rental is below the market rate for comparable facilities, another tenant may be willing to pay cash to assume the lease. The Chapter 11 firm can assign its lease in this manner, providing the new tenant is capable of fulfilling its obligation under the lease."

• Chapter 11 can be used to void onerous contracts for goods and services.

"Take the company that orders $5 million worth of materials only to find that it cannot afford to pay for the goods," says a bankruptcy consultant for Touche Ross, the national accounting firm. "If the company enters into a bankruptcy proceeding whereby it agrees to pay its creditors 15 cents on the dollar, its liability may be reduced from $5 million to 15 percent of the supplier's projected gross profit on the sale. Figuring a 20 percent profit margin, the debtor's liability would be only $150,000.

"But there are caveats. Bankruptcies are time-consuming and they carry substantial professional fees. In general, a company must be suffering from a series of problems, rather than a single onerous contract, to gain more benefits from the bankruptcy than it costs."

Review bankruptcy options with an attorney experienced in this legal specialty.

59

How to Protect Against Rising Interest Rates

O F all the costs of doing business, the cost of money may be the least predictable. Because business borrowing floats with prevailing interest rates, changes in the prime rate can bring changes in debt service and profitability. A one-point spurt in the prime can cost companies thousands in incremental interest.

With leading economists predicting that roller coaster interest rates will continue throughout the decade, many borrowers fear that they will be held hostage by every jump in the prime. But this need not be true. There is a way to insulate small companies from the ravaging effects of high interest rates.

"Management can protect against volatile interest rates by hedging with interest rate futures," says Harvey D. Moskowitz, national director of accounting and auditing for Seidman & Seidman, CPAs. "No one is certain that interest rates will rise, but companies that are highly leveraged and locked into their prices may want to consider hedging as a tool for stabilizing interest costs. In this way, a company could set selling prices with reasonable confidence that it will be protected against higher interest rates during the period."

Interest rate futures work much like commodity futures for tangible goods such as wheat and pork bellies. They are contracts to buy or sell financial instruments, such as U.S. Treasury bonds or Treasury bills, at a later date. The contracts are secured with relatively small cash payments and actual delivery of the bills rarely takes place.

"When interest rates are expected to increase, the present rate can be locked in by selling futures contracts short," Moskowitz explains. "With such a hedge, if interest rates do in fact increase, prices of interest rate futures will decline and the short position will be closed out at a profit, offsetting the increased borrowing costs."

Seidman & Seidman offers the following example of how a company can stabilize its cost of money by hedging with interest rate futures.

Company X has high short-term borrowings during its fall and winter manufacturing season. These funds are usually repaid by July 1, after the year's production has been sold. During July, the company must determine its selling prices for the fall season. Because of the seasonal borrowings, interest is a key cost factor. During July 1983 the interest rate for the company's line of credit is 11 percent. Management projects average borrowings through the season of about $5 million and expects interest rates to increase but cannot predict when or by how much.

The hedge is accomplished by selling in July 1983 fifty contracts to deliver $5 million of long-term Treasury bonds in June 1984 at $74 (a yield of about 11.3 percent). The value of the contracts is $3.7 million. If interest rates are higher in June 1984, when management expects to close out its hedge, it can then buy fifty contracts to receive

$5 million of Treasury bonds in July 1984. Because the price of the bonds drops as interest rates increase, the cost to the company in purchasing the contracts would be lower (perhaps $3,575,000 on a price of $71.50) than its short position, enabling it to close out that position at a profit. It has earned about $125,000 on the difference between the cost of the contract to cover the short position ($3,575,000) and the proceeds from the short sale ($3.7 million).

"If the prime rate had climbed from 11 percent to an average of 14 percent during the period," Moskowitz notes, "the company's interest costs based on $5 million average borrowings would have increased by about $125,000, which is offset by the profits from hedging. If interest rates had dropped, this would not have been particularly damaging because a loss in the hedge would be offset by lower borrowing costs."

One caveat is that contract price changes of Treasury bonds may not vary in direct proportion to prime rate changes. As a result, trading profits may not compensate for higher interest costs.

"It is best to match the company interest exposure with financial instruments of similar maturities," says a consultant with the Chicago Mercantile Exchange, one of the major markets for interest rate futures. "For a small firm's line of credit, I would recommend ninety-day contracts for Treasury bills or certificates of deposit."

Work with an experienced financial adviser in devising and monitoring hedge strategies. Futures contracts may be purchased from stock or commodities brokers.

60

Decision Trees Help You Manage Better

S UCCESSFUL business owners learn to see the forest *and* the trees. They keep one eye on the big picture and the other on daily events. It's a delicate balance that keeps the company on target and pointed toward long-range goals.

Mastering this double vision can be made easier by the use of decision trees. This little-known management tool breaks down the business owner's actions into a series of interrelated events. He sees both the immediate and the projected bottom line impact of every move before committing to a course of action.

"Decision trees are like road maps showing the paths leading to a decision and the consequences likely to occur once the decision is made," says a management consultant specializing in small business. "They give entrepreneurs the wisdom of hindsight—not 20/20 hindsight but it sure beats a stab in the dark.

"In every business, every day, the owner has to answer the question 'what if?' What if I open a new branch, will sales go up by 5 percent or 500 percent? What if I take on a new product, will it help or hinder existing lines? And what if I borrow money, will it generate growth or just greater debt service? Decision trees help to answer 'what ifs?' before the branch is opened, before the product is introduced and before the money is borrowed."

Consider the following guidelines for using a simplified form of decision trees:

• When faced with a business decision, management should make a list of the alternative courses of action and the resulting consequences, assigning to each a likelihood of occurrence and a projected dollar value.

It is best to keep this simple. The decision to open a new branch, for example, can affect a small business in many ways, from employee morale to the need for plate glass insurance. But in developing decision trees, the owner is advised to consider only key factors such as the impact on sales, cash flow, and profits. He should assign projected values to each of these items, comparing the results for opening a branch at location A, location B, or both.

• These numbers can then be plugged into a microcomputer program designed to do computer modeling. The computer performs the hundreds of calculations required to project the impact of the various options on the company's performance.

"Packaged software is now available to assist in this kind of modeling," the consultant notes. "Those that don't have computers can use timesharing services. There's even a value if the business owner never gets to the computer modeling phase. By simply studying the impact of business decisions before they are made, and by working through several options in advance, he is likely to reduce risks and achieve improved operating results."

Adds a vice-president of Arthur D. Little, Inc., management consultants: "Decision trees are a general approach to planning under uncertainties. More than any set formula, they are a way of thinking."

In a typical case of decision tree planning, ABC Wholesalers is asked to handle a new brand of a type of product that has not been selling well. The manufacturer is convinced that the new brand has improved features that will make it the first big winner in the field.

ABC is faced with the "what ifs?" of taking on the brand. What if the manufacturer's sales projections are way off? What if a competitor takes on the product, increasing its market share at ABC's expense? What will happen to ABC's bottom line?

"A decision tree model may show that there's a 65 percent chance of having moderate success with the new brand, a 25 percent chance of breaking even, and a 10 percent chance of losing a lot of money," Wright adds. "Management can make a more informed decision."

Consultants, computer experts, and accountants can help design and analyze decision trees.

61
Umbrellas Can Protect Your Assets

SOMETIMES the trappings of success turn out to be the targets of litigation. Sailboats, summer homes, and shares of company stock make for plum settlements in high-stakes law suits. Owners can find their most valuable assets seized by the courts.

This scenario is painfully familiar to thousands of small-business owners and self-employed professionals. As high-income individuals—often with substantial business and personal assets—they are subject to multimillion-dollar lawsuits for everything from traffic accidents to household injuries. Should legal settlements exceed their automobile, homeowner, and other insurance coverage, cash in the bank or the German sports car may have to be surrendered to foot the bill.

"People tend to sue more readily and for larger sums when the subject of the suit is a person of means," says an executive vice-president of the Insurance Company of North America. "There is simply more to gain. The affluent business owner, for example, has substantial resources. He can always be forced to sell shares of stock in his own company to settle the claim."

But there is a way to protect against this. Umbrella liability policies pick up where standard coverage leaves off. For as little as $100 per year, the successful entrepreneur or professional can build in a $1 million buffer against the loss of personal assets.

"While most business owners protect their corporate assets with commercial umbrella policies, many fail to afford themselves similar protection with personal umbrellas," the executive adds. "That can be a terrible mistake. Why risk the fruits of success when they can be guarded for so small a premium?"

Umbrella policies generally contain the following provisions:

• Coverage provides for attorneys' fees and related legal costs in defending against negligence suits. In a typical case, this can total $10,000 or more. Should the individual be uninsured against the type of claim filed, the costs would have to be paid out of pocket.

• Umbrella coverage is available in million-dollar denominations with typical annual premiums of $100 for $1 million and $175 for $2 million.

• Many policies provide coverage that extends beyond routine physical injuries to include certain claims for mental anguish, mental injury, defamation of character, and invasion of the rights of privacy.

• The insured is protected against actual damages including medical expenses, loss of income, property damage, and pain and suffering.

"One of our policyholders, a yacht owner, was entertaining friends on his boat when it caught fire," says an assistant secretary of the Hartford Insurance Group. "They were barbecuing and some of the flames spread to the deck. Several of the guests were injured and they sued the owner for more than a half million dollars. His umbrella policy covered all of his personal liability."

Still, there are gaps in umbrella coverage. Policies do not cover business-related claims; these must be protected by commercial policies. Also, should settlement costs exceed the policy maximum, the insured will face personal liability for the excess amount. This is why care must be taken to purchase a large-enough policy.

The best approach is to seek the advice of an accountant or other financial adviser in determining the amount of umbrella protection required to provide adequate coverage. Then shop around among the insurance carriers for the best mix of coverage terms, deductibles, and premiums.

62
Licensing Can Put E.T. to Work for You

C AN small business find happiness in partnership
with E.T.? Do the Smurfs have the secrets to
earning greater profits? For companies willing to
learn the ins and outs of licensing, the answer may be yes.

Licensing harnesses the enormous appeal of television
and film characters, designer labels, and status insignia, and
puts them to work for a wide range of commercial
products. When the process works well, run-of-the-mill
merchandise gains a new appeal, boosting its performance
in the marketplace.

It works like this. A small manufacturer of children's
clothing finds that sales are sluggish and that big competitors are eating into his market share. To fight back, he
signs a deal with the owners of a popular trademark who
allow him to use reproductions of cartoon characters on his
garments. Suddenly, his apparel line turns from routine to
red hot.

"Licensing is booming," says the executive vice-president of Hamilton Projects, marketing consultants. "Companies want and need a competitive advantage and many turn to licensing. The concept is used most often by manufacturers but it has application for a wide range of small businesses including retailers and mail order houses."

Companies seeking licensing agreements must apply to the trademark owners of their agents. If these licensors believe that the applicant company is capable of representing its image and of selling a substantial volume of goods, permission will be granted to use the desired logo, symbol, or other promotional identification. In return, the licensee agrees to pay a royalty—generally 6 percent to 10 percent—on the wholesale value of the goods sold.

Licensing agreements may be exclusives, granting the user sole rights to the promotional symbol; limited exclusives, which cover a specific product or geographic region; or non-exclusives, which offer no competitive protection.

"Although small businesses rarely have the marketing clout to gain full exclusives, there are exceptions," the VP adds. "The E.T. doll went not to the largest manufacturer in the field but to one the licensor believed was best suited to produce quality goods."

Licensing carries risks as well as rewards. Consider the following:

• In most cases, licensees must commit themselves to a minimum royalty payment. This advance, based on projected sales, is generally paid 50 percent on signing of the licensing agreement and the balance at a specified accounting period. The sum is owed even if sales fall below projections.

• Promotional symbols have brief life cycles, moving in and out of popularity like shooting stars. Companies paying substantial advances for properties that have peaked may find that licensing produces little more than red ink.

• Small firms seeking the rights to very popular licenses may be forced to expand their production to meet anticipated demand. Should the trademark quickly lose its appeal, management may be unable to recover its capital investment.

"I have used licenses for many years and my experience with them varies across the lot," says the chairman of a company that manufactures patches and emblems. "They can give your product a real boost but only if the license is properly policed. If counterfeiters are allowed to crowd the market with fakes, the license is useless. The best approach is to work with a licensor with a good track record in policing its properties."

Ask trade associations for help in tracking down licensors and marketing firms active in this specialty.

63

New Fringe Benefit Plan Aids Company and Employees

S MALL companies burdened by high pension costs may find relief in an obscure fringe benefit plan that simultaneously reduces salaries, cuts taxes, and provides for employee retirement. Management, workers, and the corporation stand to gain.

Through 401 (k) plans (named after the section of the Revenue Code that authorizes them), companies can establish vehicles for retirement income funded all or in part by employees. To encourage this self-help approach, the government reduces the employee's taxable income by the amount of his 401 (k) contribution.

"This is a major advantage over traditional qualified benefit plans," says a partner with Hewitt Associates, a consulting firm specializing in fringe benefit plans. "It means that contributions are made with pre-tax rather than after-tax dollars, thus helping the employee pay for his retirement plan. A worker earning $20,000 per year and making a $3,000 contribution to a 401 (k) only need report

$17,000 of income. The tax saving partially offsets the cost of the contribution."

The 401 (k) plans—also known as Salary Reduction Plans—offer these additional benefits:

• Lump sum distributions taken at retirement or at the termination of employment are eligible for ten-year forward-averaging tax treatment. To arrive at this figure, the tax on one tenth of the distribution is multiplied by ten. Because the tax is levied on a small part of the income and because the distribution is not mingled with other earnings, the marginal tax rate remains low for all but the largest settlements.

"Were the distribution treated as ordinary income—as it is with lump sums taken from Individual Retirement Accounts—it would be combined with salary, dividends, and interest the taxpayer earned from other sources," the Hewitt partner explains. "This means the distribution would be subject to a higher marginal tax rate.

"For example, assume a married taxpayer (in the 30 percent marginal tax bracket while employed, 15 percent at retirement) receives a lump sum distribution of $125,150. His tax would be $55,400 with an IRA but only $23,300 with a 401 (k). That makes for a savings of $32,100."

• Maximum contributions to a 401 (k) far exceed the $2,000 ceiling on IRAs. Subject to anti-discrimination rules which prevent the owners and highest paid employees from gaining a lopsided share of the benefits, 401 (k) annual contributions can be as high as $30,000 or 25 percent of an employee's compensation, whichever is less.

• Premature withdrawals—which are allowed in cases of hardship—are not subject to the 10 percent penalty imposed on IRAs.

• Employees may contribute to both IRAs and 401 (k) plans; corporations may offer 401 (k) plans in place of or in addition to other qualified plans.

• Small-business owners may delegate 401 (k) investment responsibilities to their employees, permitting participants to select investments best suited for their personal goals.

Prototype plans approved by the Internal Revenue Service are available for small-business participation from benefits consultants, insurance companies, mutual funds, and investment firms.

"Companies using our plans can give their employees the option of investing in eight different mutual funds," says an assistant vice-president of Scudder, Stevens & Clark, investment advisers. "For a management fee, we design the plan, manage the funds, and report on their performance."

Adds Hewitt Associates, "The 401 (k) plans are simple to start, simple to administer and are a good low-cost option for emerging firms that want to provide fringe benefits at little or no corporate expense. Companies that don't have the resources to fund pension plans can use the 401 (k) as a viable substitute."

Explore the pros and cons of 401 (k) plans with an accountant, tax attorney, or benefits consultant.

64

Trade Shows Can Boost Business Sales

JUST when small business needs a marketing work-horse, trade shows step up to fill the role. These high-octane events offer the power of numbers plus the appeal of one-on-one contacts. Companies adept at trade show presentations can walk away with a basket of new business and a wealth of promising leads.

Trade shows are forums for the display and sale of related goods and services. They bring together an industry's major manufacturers, retailers, and middlemen. By participating as exhibitors, small-business owners can touch base with a wide range of potential customers. Some exhibitors claim that a single trade show produces more business than 100 sales calls.

"Trade shows are today's most cost-effective method of marketing," says an official with the Trade Show Bureau, the industry's research arm. "A McGraw-Hill survey shows that the cost of a standard industrial sales call has skyrocketed to $178. Compare that to $66.88 for a trade show contact. By attending trade shows, small business can drum up new sales at a relatively modest expense."

The vice-president of a giftware importing and distributing firm agrees.

"Trade shows now account for 27 percent of our sales volume. Our experience with them has been so positive that we've gradually increased our participation to about 60 shows a year. The biggest plus is that we can show customers our entire product line at a single viewing. You can't do that on a standard sales call. There's not enough room in the sample case. At trade shows we display our full collection and we sell it."

But there's more to it than simply setting up a booth and writing orders. Experts recommend the following guidelines for successful trade show participation:

• Ask business asscociates or trade groups for a list of major shows in your industry. Contact the show managers, asking them to provide you with attendance profiles of the past year's events. Select the shows that attract the best prospects for your goods and services.

• Stay away from trade shows that are being launched for the first time. There is no way to gauge their performance, and applicants risk paying deposits for shows that may not get off the ground.

• Once you have selected a show, negotiate for the best floor space. Experienced exhibitors favor positions by the front door, in the middle of the exhibit hall, and near food concessions. Display fees, generally the same for all locations on the selling floor, do vary from show to show. Figure a range of $5 to $25 per square foot.

• Conduct advance advertising and publicity campaigns to inform customers of your participation. This builds attendance, which in turn generates more orders.

"Don't expect the business to fall in your lap," says an executive with George Little Management, Inc., trade show producers. "Successful exhibitors do extensive pre-show publicity and direct mail promotions to ensure a substantial turnout. When companies fail at trade shows, inadequate publicity is often the reason."

• Create a display that stands out in a crowd and that draws attention to the company's wares.

"Because the small business is often competing for attention with well-known corporations, it needs an attention-getting device that makes up for its relative obscurity," says a display designer. "I call it a hook. For a maker of boating winches, we built a working model of a winch hoisting an anchor."

Professionally designed displays can be produced for about $400 per running foot. Some designers insist on a ten-foot minimum.

"Displays must be functional as well as creative," the designer adds. "They must have a little area set aside for private conversations. Once the exhibitor attracts the prospect, he should have some facility for doing business. All it takes is a couple of chairs and a plexiglass screen. Successful trade show exhibitors never forget that they are there to write orders."

65
Starting a Group IRA

NOW that Individual Retirement Accounts are for everyone, employers can help everyone benefit from them. Group plans encouraging employee participation are available through major banks, brokerage houses, and investment firms.

The Economic Recovery Act of 1981 expanded IRA eligibility to include all workers, even those covered by company pension plans, and boosted the maximum annual contribution from 15 percent of income or a limit of $1,500 to 100 percent of compensation or $2,000, whichever is less. Contributions to IRAs are tax deductible and funds accumulate tax-free until they are withdrawn at age fifty-nine and one half or later.

Millions of Americans are jumping on the IRA bandwagon, using the device as an additional way to shield income from taxes. Small-business owners can facilitate this move by arranging for group IRA plans that make participation as simple as signing on the dotted line.

"Once they agree to invest with us, we handle all the administrative responsibilities of the IRA," says a vice-president of Fidelity Management Group, an investment firm. "Each employee in the group plan gets his own account and his own reports on the account's performance. We handle billing, maintenance, and reporting."

Payments through group plans are made in any of three ways: a lump sum contribution covering all participating employees including the owner; a payroll deduction system that automatically subtracts from each check a specified amount for IRA contributions; or an electronic funds transfer that directs a set amount each month from the employees' checking accounts to the group plan investment firm. In most cases, plan sponsors arrange and implement the payment system.

One of the real pluses of group IRAs is that the small-company's management does not have fudiciary responsibility for it. Employees make their own investment decisions, such as switching funds from one investment option in the plan to another. A key attraction of the group plans is that many offer a wide range of investment vehicles.

"Participants in our group IRAs can choose among virtually all of the investments we offer," says a vice-president responsible for retirement plans and services for Merrill Lynch Pierce Fenner & Smith. "Employees can choose to invest in stocks, bonds, money market funds, mutual funds, and real estate limited partnerships. Just about the only things we exclude them from are commodities, tax-exempt instruments, and most options trading.

"Because each employee has his own account in the plan, he can change as often as he wishes from one type of investment to another. Should a shift in the economy favor securities, he can invest in stocks. Three months later he can change directions and invest all or part of his IRA in bonds.

Although there is great flexibility in these plans, we suggest that participants take a long-term view rather than base investment decisions on daily events."

Employers may serve as passive conduits for their employees' IRA investments or may make the contributions for them as tax-deductible fringe benefits. Contributions may be limited to key executives or sales personnel or may be made for every employee in the firm. The non-discrimination rules that are built into other pension plans do not apply to IRAs.

Pension consultants can help small firms decide whether to arrange for group plans and if so how to incorporate them into a total benefits package.

"We analyze all the variables," explains a partner with Hewitt Associates, benefits consultants. "Sometimes we'll advise a company to start a group IRA, but in other cases, where employee interest seems low, we'll suggest that management just inform employees of what they can do on their own and leave it at that."

66

Focus Groups Help You Read Your Customers' Minds

I T'S been said that the key to a successful small business is the owner's ability to read his customers' minds. By knowing what they want before they ask for it, management can put the right products and services in place, ready for sale, long before the competition catches on.

There's a way to stimulate this mind reading without buying a crystal ball or acquiring the powers of extrasensory perception. An obscure market research technique—known as focus groups—allows executives to eavesdrop on consumers, learning their tastes and preferences on everything from merchandise selection to credit terms.

"Focus groups generally bring together ten to twenty consumers for the purpose of discussing their attitudes toward the marketplace," says the president of The Research Department, a New York–based market research firm.

"The topic of conversation for each session can be as broad as an entire product category or as narrow as a

specific brand name. Within these guidelines—established
by the company sponsoring the research—the group
moderator elicits from the participants their attitudes, likes,
dislikes and personal experiences.

"For example, assume a small food company wants to
enter the salad dressing market by creating an innovative
product that can compete against the market leaders.
Management believes that a cottage cheese–based dressing
will appeal to today's diet-conscious consumers. But before
investing in production and promotion, the firm conducts
focus groups to determine if consumers are equally
enthusiastic. Would they buy the product? What name
would work best? How about the packaging? Focus groups
can provide helpful information on all of this."

Focus-group participants—who are recruited by the
market researchers—may include current users of the
company's products, users of competitive products, or those
who've yet to make their first purchase in the product
category. It is best to divide the various segments into
separate consumer groups.

"All sorts of variations are possible," the researcher
continues. "With those consumers loyal to competitors, you
can determine what it will take to win them over. With
those who consciously avoid your product, you can find out
how to get back in their good graces. And for those first
entering the market, you can position yourself to get their
business and keep it."

Focus-group sessions generally run for two hours, the
participants are paid from $20 to $200 each and management obtains a comprehensive report on the findings.
Typical fees range from $1,500 to $3,000 per session, which
covers all costs.

"It's a worthwhile investment, considering how much it
can help you make or save on your business operations,"
says one entrepreneur. "In planning my company, which

markets hearing aids through special diagnostic centers, we found that consumers feared our facilities would be cold and impersonal. By knowing this in advance, we were able to come up with a design that imparted a cozy, friendly feeling. Consumers have responded to it very favorably. The focus groups were a real help."

But there are limitations. Because the groups are not based on scientific samples, their attitudes cannot be viewed as a mirror image of the broader market. What's more, the reliability of focus-group data varies with the experience and the expertise of the various market research firms. Advertising agencies can recommend reputable outfits.

67

How to Buy a Small-Business Computer

FOR small business, deciding to buy a computer is easier than deciding which computer to buy. The market is jammed with a dizzying array of computer brand names, each with a slew of models, features, and accessories. Overwhelmed by the choices, many shoppers buy the first thing they see or buy nothing at all. But there is a better way.

"It is especially important for the computer novice—the person setting out to buy the first microcomputer for his business or professional practice—to conduct the search armed with objective criteria," says a small-business computer specialist with Touche Ross & Co., CPAs. "Without this, he will be buffeted by the competing claims of manufacturers' sales representatives. Just when a unit sounds like a perfect match for his business, a salesman will come through the door and say that unit is obsolete. It goes on and on.

"The bottom line is that manufacturers' claims are biased, thus the importance of independent criteria. Knowing what to look for can help to sort out the puff from the pertinent. Suddenly the market doesn't seem all that confusing."

Consider the following guidelines for purchasing small-business computers:

• Recognize that you are buying two different components, hardware and software. Reverse the traditional pattern: shop for software first and then search for compatible hardware.

"Keep in mind that the computer itself, the hardware, is just a box," the consultant warns. "It's the software that can be tailored to your company's needs and that plays the biggest role in automating your operations. Give it priority treatment."

• Look for a software package that provides for "integrated data." This means that the information generated on one aspect of the business, such as order entries, automatically adjusts the database on inventories and accounts receivable. This boosts efficiency and gives management a wide-angle view of the business.

• Favor those dealers or manufacturers with local service outlets. Once your company is automated, delays in servicing can foul up your customer service systems and management controls.

• Pay special attention to features that make the computer easy to learn and operate. For example, check that the computer clearly signals when a mistake is made and that it allows the user to make a correction.

• Make certain that the manufacturer offers comprehensive training manuals as well as live instruction for employees and management. Some dealers hold regularly scheduled classes on computer operations.

• Check with trade associations to determine which computer systems are favored by others in your industry. A number of leading manufacturers have developed systems geared to the needs of specialized businesses such as retailing, finance, legal, and many others.

• Be sure the system is expandable. A small-business computer should be able to grow along with the user company, taking on additional memory and terminals as the firm's database expands.

• Insist on a minimum ninety-day guarantee on hardware parts and labor.

• Ask for a working demonstration of both the hardware and software. Make this a trial run of the system's on-the-job performance.

"A good test is to have the sales representative demonstrate the system's general ledger capabilities by entering data from your company's books," says a senior staffer with the consulting firm of Arthur D. Little. "Check his results with a small task, like entering part of your chart of accounts. His performance will tell a lot more about the computer than you can learn from a brochure or a sales pitch."

68

How to Rent a Store

THE great success stories of modern retailing started out with a small shop and a good location. Merchants seeking to duplicate that success today must do much the same. Renting the right store at the right price is still the first step.

But it is not as easy as it sounds. Nailing down a good retail store involves a thousand and one considerations, including costs, location, and lease terms. Many retailers simply don't know what to look for.

"They go by instinct alone and that's not good enough," says Michael Hirschfeld, chairman of Garrick-Aug Associates, brokers and consultants specializing in retail rentals. "It's not much better than judging a used car by kicking the tires. Unless merchants recognize the opportunities and the pitfalls in store rentals, they'll make disastrous mistakes on this most important aspect of their business activities."

Experts recommend adhering to the following guidelines for renting retail space:

• Do not accept the stated rental at face value. Virtually all rents are negotiable, with some owners willing to go well below the initial quote. Most landlords set the first figure artificially high in expectation of a negotiated settlement down the road. Figure a downward margin of approximately 15 percent.

• Be on the lookout for especially attractive bargains during recessions. Many property owners are strapped for cash and are eager to accept rental deals they may have once rejected. Commercial real estate brokers can tip off tenants to these opportunities.

• Look for ways to operate with a minimum amount of space. Cut back on less profitable merchandise lines and service areas and organize the remaining sections with the most efficient displays. This can slash a merchant's square footage requirements by 20 percent or more and can make it possible to rent a smaller store. The savings go right to the bottom line.

"One common mistake is to rent much more space than the merchant needs so that he'll have room to expand for the next ten years," Hirschfeld adds. "That simply burdens the present with dreams of the future. By overloading the company with a great deal of excess space and overhead, the retailer makes it harder for his company to survive for another ten years. Should the firm be successful, chances are good it will be able to find additional space when it needs it."

• Merchants seeking to serve a large market area should consider renting two smaller shops at different locations rather than one large store. This doubles the firm's exposure and spreads its risks without doubling the cost of doing business. Some of the company's fixed costs can be apportioned to both units. One school of thought says open a shop at a downtown location and another at a suburban mall.

• Be aware that many retail leases have kickers that boost the space costs well above the base price per square foot. Periodic escalators may call for percentage increases every few years, and shopping center leases may demand a percentage of the merchant's sales. Compute these costs into the amount of the lease.

• Do not be misled by published figures citing a mall or shopping center's average square foot rentals. The large anchor stores often get sweetheart deals to lure them into the center, thus pushing down the average rent. Small merchants may wind up paying 50 percent more per square foot than their giant neighbors.

• Try to avoid signing for the lease personally. Put the lease in the name of a corporation. Have a lawyer and a CPA review the terms of the lease and get their opinion before making a commitment.

• Professional corporations, the newest entrants in the retail market, may follow the same guidelines.

69

Roadmap Program Can Be "Your Man in Washington"

THE U.S. Commerce Department—Uncle Sam's major link with the business community—is helping small companies cut through the red tape that clutters official Washington. Requests for information, loans, and licenses are guided through the bureaucracy, speeding the response time and improving the odds of success.

It's all part of the Roadmap program, a service based on the theory that "it's not what you know that counts but who you know." Self-employed men and women in need of federal government assistance are put in touch with those officials best positioned to handle the matter promptly.

"Big corporations retain a local staff or a Washington law firm to look after their affairs in the nation's capital," says an official with the Commerce Department's Office of Business Liaison. "Roadmap's major objective is to help those firms that cannot afford the luxury of private representation."

To make use of the program, business owners and professionals call the Roadmap hotline at (202) 337-3176 or write to the Office of Business Liaison, Commerce Department, Washington, DC 20230. It is best to describe the problem or request in detail, citing dates, dollar amounts, and the type of business activity. Program coordinators will either deal with the matter on the spot, refer it to a well-placed contact in the federal government, or ask for time to do some research. In most cases, a return call is made within twenty-four hours of the initial request.

Roadmap differs from other government information services in that it is geared to the needs of the entire business community. Commerce Department staffers route requests for assistance through all federal agencies with jurisdiction in commercial transactions. The program will not, however, work with state governments and does not serve as a company's advocate in proceedings with the federal government.

Companies can call on Roadmap to:

• Gather information on how to start a business. For example, should a caller need special help in launching a minority-owned business, names and numbers of Small Business Administration experts in this area will be provided. Program coordinators will also tell where to write for government publications on small-business management.

• Identify sources of small-company loans and government grants. Dozens of federal agencies offer various types of financial assistance. Determining the best source can take a bit of detective work. Roadmap's familiarity with the rules and requirements for financial aid can help to narrow the options.

• Clarify federal laws and regulations. This is especially important for newly enacted legislation.

"Companies may have to make major decisions before a law is fully explained in the press," the Roadmap official adds. "In that case, we try to put the business owners in touch with the politicians most closely associated with the legislation. Their staff members can often clarify the issues and help management make more informed decisions."

"When one of our customers ran into red tape with a Food and Drug Administration official, we almost lost a $100,000 order," says an executive with a company that produces weighing equipment. "The customer couldn't get approval to package 80,000 pounds of cheese that he wanted to sell. We called the Roadmap people and they got the problem resolved within forty-eight hours. That saved the order and the customer's loyalty."

Spot checks of the Roadmap program reveal that the quality of the service varies with the mood of the person handling the call. Sometimes the response is diligent and thorough; at other times it is careless and impatient. Those business owners who receive poor treatment should demand to speak to a supervisor.

70

Strategic Planning Opens Doors to the Future

T HE future. To small business, it is change and continuity, challenge and opportunity, the predictable and the unknown. Many fear it; others find ways to limit the risks and to improve the prospects for long-term success.

One risk-reducing technique often associated with major corporations—strategic planning—can be equally effective in helping small companies plan for and influence the future.

"Strategic planning allows management to capitalize on emerging opportunities rather than just reacting to problems," says a partner with Seidman & Seidman, CPAs. "Just how this can help a company shape its future is illustrated by the experience of three entrepreneurs who purchased a company that manufactures awnings. Upon assuming control of the business, they discovered inefficiencies in material handling and employee productivity. Because these problems were attributable to the company's seasonal sales patterns, they were unlikely to go away on their own.

"But through enlightened use of strategic planning, the owners were able to reverse a gradual deterioration of the business while simultaneously establishing a base for future expansion. This was accomplished by diversifying into growth markets that were complementary to the company's skills and resources, thus offsetting the seasonal effect. Their success can serve as an inspiration for many small businesses."

Major components of strategic planning include:

• An honest appraisal of the company's strengths and weaknesses. Frank discussions with employees, managers, and external consultants should answer such questions as: Does the company have a good reputation in the market-place? Are its products or services competitively priced? Does management have access to adequate credit?

Negative findings indicate the weak points in need of corrective action.

• Defining the entrepreneur's goals to ensure that the firm's policies and practices are in sync with the chief executive's underlying objectives. Business owners seeking maximum personal income and company-paid perks will favor practices different from those building the bottom line in anticipation of a sale or merger.

• Setting company goals that are realistic and achievable within a reasonable period of time. Goals identified as "impossible" will not motivate employees. It is also important to express operating targets in specific terms. It is better to aim for, say, pretax income of 10 percent than to shoot for "higher profits."

• Developing strategies to achieve the company's goals. Here, experts recommend brainstorming sessions involving representatives from all functions active in producing and marketing the company's products and services.

"It was at this step that the awning entrepreneurs had an important revelation," the Seidman & Seidman partner explains. "As veterans of the sporting goods industry, they recognized similarities between the production of awnings and that of high quality canvas and nylon tents. Without much of an investment, they could enter the tent market, open an avenue for future growth, and solve some of their existing problems. It served all of their needs simultaneously, but it would not have come to their attention without strategic planning."

• Monitoring performance to determine that the company is meeting its objectives. The strategic plan must be revised from time to time to adjust for competitive, technological, and internal developments.

"Change, though inevitable, need not be feared," the Seidman partner adds. "Not as long as the company keeps its strategic plan under constant scrutiny, modifies it when necessary, and uses it as a tool for dealing with the future— the unknown."

Management consultants and general practice accountants can help to design and implement strategic plans.

71

Self-Help Groups Help Merchants Help Themselves

B USINESS helping business. That's the concept behind a group-based consulting plant that gives independent store owners the power of numbers. By working together, merchants replace competition with cooperation.

The concept dates back to 1922 when Scull and Co., a consulting firm specializing in retail clients, launched the first of its self-help groups. By creating networks of small stores over the years, the firm has widened local merchants' horizons, enabling group members to learn from each other.

"There's no more valuable information on how to run a small business than the combined experience of those engaged in it," says Scull president Robert L. Huppelsberg. "The problem is, the laws of the marketplace demand that entrepreneurs spend all of their time battling each other rather than sharing their wisdom. We've developed a system that allows merchants to remain competitive in their trading areas but cooperative in their consulting groups."

A partner active in national retail practice for Touche Ross, CPAs, agrees. "Their service to small retailers is unique and extremely beneficial. Peer contact enables the participants to learn from one another—to be better business owners."

It works like this:

Scull members are assigned to work with groups of merchants active in the same retail specialty but in different geographic markets. A jeweler, for example, works with other jewelers based outside of his sales territory. Because members share common goals without sharing customers, they are open to the free exchange of ideas. Groups meet semiannually to report on their business performance.

"This is a three- to five-day conference during which members report their sales figures, profit margins, and experiences with new branches, merchandising techniques, and promotions," Huppelsberg explains. "Through this interchange, the merchants pick up strategies for making their own companies more successful. Recently, one member described how he used a hot air balloon to promote his store, selling advertising messages on the sides of the balloon to cover the costs of the campaign. And a piano merchant recounted the steps he took to conduct a warehouse sale featuring 200 pianos displayed in a rented armory."

Between meetings, Scull maintains the flow of information through these member services:

• An information exchange provides group members with operating data on each of the participating stores. Reports cover basic sales information, chart performance by product line and price category, and also include comprehensive information on store expenses. Data is

structured to reveal key retail yardsticks such as sales per
square foot and average gross sale. Each member is privy
to the others' data but in coded form to prevent leaks to
competitors.

The information exchange is designed to help
merchants identify trends and to compare their results with
the group's performance. Should a store owner experience
a drastic decline in the sales of mid-priced dresses while
others in the group are reporting sales gains in the same
product line, the disparity is a red flag, alerting the
merchant to the need for corrective action.

"Running a small business is a very lonely experience,"
says one clothing store owner. "You have to make decisions
yourself, without the benefit of staff advisers. But the group
fills this void by giving you access to your peers. It's helped
my business substantially. Since joining a Scull group four
years ago, we've expanded from one store to three."

• A computerized information center gives members
access to a database of retail information from inventory
systems to cash management techniques.

Fees for Scull's services generally range from $1,200 to
$2,000 per year (this may be higher for larger stores) plus a
$100 initiation fee. Merchants may contact the company at
230 West 41st Street, New York, NY 10036.

Although members seem to be pleased with the
program, there are drawbacks. Merchant presentations can
stress business successes rather than failures. While this may
pamper egos, it does not help colleagues avoid similar
pitfalls. Also, because group members must work together,
they may avoid making pointed criticisms of one another's
stores. That's like sweeping problems under the rug. Some
merchants may find that they are better served by
independent consultants.

72

Sharing the Equity Pie Keeps Employees Focused on the Bottom Line

WHEN small business divides the equity pie—giving ownership to employees as well as the boss—morale and productivity soar. Those with a vested interest in the bottom line work overtime to cut costs and boost productivity.

"Spreading the wealth makes for a more successful and competitive firm," says a partner of the Pittsburgh-based law firm of Buchanan Ingersoll. "Because they have a personal stake in their company's performance, employees with stock or other equity interests are more loyal, inventive and committed to achieving management's objectives. Also, the opportunity to share in the equity can attract talented employees that might otherwise be recruited by major corporations.

"At the very least, management should offer equity to the handful of key executives most valuable to the firm. Because the non-discrimination rules that govern qualified retirement plans do not apply to equity arrangements, the company can fashion any type of equity package that best suits its needs."

The following equity sharing techniques can be used singly or in combination with others:

• Companies in the earliest stages of development can sell shares of stock to employees at the current market price. Because start-up firms are considered high-risk ventures, share values are often negligible, perhaps $1 or less. Employees can buy in low and gain handsomely as the shares appreciate.

"Equity sharing plans should meet three fundamental tests," the attorney says. "The employees should be able to buy in without making major investments, the stock should be capable of appreciating significantly over the years and the shares should be eligible for capital gain treatment when they are ultimately sold."

• Companies further along the growth curve—whose shares have already appreciated substantially—can allow employees to buy in at opportune prices through incentive stock options. In a typical example, selected employees are granted options to buy 1,000 shares of the company's stock, anytime in the next five years, at the current $5 market price. Should the shares fail to rise beyond that price, the option need not be exercised.

On the other hand, should the company's growth propel the stock price significantly higher, say to $25 a share, the employees can buy the 1,000 shares at $5 each, earning a profit of $20 per share when the stock is sold. To qualify for capital gain treatment, the shares must be held for the latter of one year after the exercise of the option or two years from the date the option was granted.

"The ability to pay only capital gain taxes, providing

the required tests are met, makes incentive stock options highly attractive to employees," says a partner with Arthur Young, the national accounting firm.

• Stock bonuses award employees with company shares when predetermined objectives such as sales or manufacturing quotas are achieved. Although employees must pay ordinary income tax equal to the stock's fair market value at the time the bonus is granted, profit on subsequent sales of the stock can qualify for capital gain treatment.

• Formula stock plans enable employees to buy shares of stock at a low market value and to postpone taxes until the shares are sold.

"With this approach, the company establishes a formula for valuing its shares, say twelve times earnings," the attorney explains, "and sells stock to the employee according to this formula. At the same time, the company enters into an agreement with the employee to buy back the shares at one or more future dates, with the price to be based on the same multiple of earnings.

"Assume that when the stock is first bought by the employee, earnings are ten cents a share. If earnings subsequently rise to $1 a share, the employee stands to make $10.80 on each share of stock he owns. Because value was originally placed on the shares, there is no tax until the stock is sold by the employee and then only at capital gain rates.

"Although the formula stock approach is relatively new and somewhat untested with the Internal Revenue Service, we believe it is the way many equity plans will work in the future."

Equity sharing involves complex tax, legal and accounting issues. Review all strategies with an experienced professional.

Following Up

You have now benefited from a wealth of cost-cutting, profit-making strategies. But your job is not over. Not as a business owner nor as a practitioner of the system we've called *The 10-Minute Entrepreneur*. Change will not allow you to rely solely on what you've learned to date. Change in tax laws, advertising techniques, technology, competition, product pricing, interest rates, economic conditions, the value of the dollar, the cost of living, the minimum wage and on and on demand that aggressive and sophisticated entrepreneurs keep searching for new loop-holes, strategies and tactics.

To do so, you must develop a network of professional and commercial contacts in position to keep you attuned to change as it occurs. This provides the competitive edge so vital to success in today's turbulent but promising markets.

Assemble the network with paid consultants—accountants, attorneys, certified financial planners, benefits consultants, and management consultants—as well as with business associates including wholesalers, suppliers, retailers, and trade representatives. Make it clear that you want the benefit of their wisdom and insights and you are willing to compensate them with fees or shared information.

Most important, maintain the regimen you have begun with *The 10-Minute Entrepreneur*. Continue to set aside a part of your day for learning and implementing action plans. Use the time to call contacts, to visit with members of your information network, to incorporate new ideas into your business operation. You will be rewarded for your discipline. You will keep apace with change.